The Sea Remains

JEAN SULIVAN

The Sea Remains

A NOVEL

Translated by ROBERT A. DONAHUE, Jr.
and JOSEPH CUNNEEN

Crossroad · New York

1989
The Crossroad Publishing Company
370 Lexington Avenue, New York, N.Y. 10017

Originally published under the title *Mais il y a la mer*
© Éditions Gallimard, 1964
English translation copyright © 1989 by The Crossroad Publishing Company
Printed in the United States of America

Library of Congress Cataloging-in-Publication Data

Sulivan, Jean.
  [Mais il y a la mer. English]
  The sea remains: a novel / Jean Sulivan; translated by Robert A.
  Donahue, Jr. and Joseph Cunneen
  p. cm.
  Translation of: Mais il y a la mer.
  ISBN 0-8245-0946-3:
  I. Title.
PQ2679.U5M313   1989
843'.914--dc19   89-31122
                                              CIP

For my mother
because she likes to tell stories

The sea is there, and who shall drain its yield?
It breeds precious as silver, ever of itself renewed,
the purple ooze wherein our garments shall be dipped.

Aeschylus, *Agamemnon*, ll. 959–60
(translated by Richard Lattimore)

1

~~~~~~

*A*nd all this because one spring, looking for a barren country, you thought this might be a place to stop.

A cove just outside Noria, close by but hidden by a hill embankment that slumps toward the sea, collapses into a chaos of boulders. No more eucalyptus, lemon, or orange groves: from here on, it's just dry, bare land. The cove forms a nearly perfect oval if you leave a gate for the sea, a narrow gully among the boulders, narrow enough to keep out the tourists and allow only the smallest boats to enter. At the other end, a single white villa, shaped like a cube, stands surrounded by a dozen pine trees which have something inhuman about them. The murmur of the sea cancels the murmur of the town and its immense rectilinear beach behind the embankment insures the silence needed for great thoughts.

Turn your head slowly to the left, look away from the sea and the sky, which at this hour of the day form an indistinct mass the color of lead. Follow a rock path that for a moment hugs the cove on the cliff, then zigzags through the boulders, the thick shrubs, the prickly pear, the agave, the tufts of burnt grass, and the bush that gives off an odor of incense—what's its name? Cross small rocky fields of some crop or other, you arrive at the village of Altata, at that height scarcely distinguishable from the russet stone. It's like a village in an abstract painting that Minka, standing just below the blue sierra, never stops working on: ocher, brick red, burnt umber.

The Altata road skirts the villa before mounting the embankment and descending to Noria, invisible yet near. You'd have to turn around to follow it and look up again to catch sight of the barrel of a gun and a helmet, which have been coming and going on the gangway for centuries, back and forth between two Moorish towers above the entrance to a sleepy fortress whose function is to swallow up free men. It is the state prison, reached by a broad, winding road. But in order to see the gun barrel, the helmet, and the Moorish towers rising to the sea over the villa, you have to walk out to the middle of the cove and turn your back on the sea.

A man is seated, perfectly still, on the second of the stone steps that mount to the terrace of the cubelike villa. His feet rest on the first step, a cane between his knees, his two joined hands pressing down on the cane's ivory knob. Now that the man has deserted his happiness and we have several days yet before the police close this house for the dying, we can examine this cane more attentively. It is of a hard, black wood, teak probably; the slightly yellowed ivory is almost transparent from having been pressed by so many old, translucent hands. It leans against the wall beside a tall, narrow clock in the vestibule of the house.

So, hands joined on the yellowed ivory knob, the bust inclined forward but face raised, a long face the color of dried figs: acute angles—the angle of the knees, the angle formed by the thighs and the bust, the angle between the upper arm and forearm, the angle of the hands joined on the cane. But the man as a whole could be inscribed in an almost perfect circle. The cove is still empty: the man's eyes raised above the chaos of boulders in the narrow gully are fixed on the motionless tumult of the leaden sea, which blends into the sky. He is waiting: the coolness, the odor of the sea flower, perhaps the child who almost always comes with the sea.

Every few minutes Doña Paca presses her long, wilted face to the window of the drawing room. All she can see is the head of the statue, cut off by the terrace.

2

The child, who has run down the hill coming from Noria, pops up like the breeze, a cloud in an open sky.

"Here, this is for the martin."

Then off he goes toward the gully, now at a gallop, now skipping, now turning cartwheels; plunging among the boulders in search of the surprises brought by the night tide; returning with his hands laden with shells, seaweed, and starfish. He goes off again to play incomprehensible games; now he's only a red-and-black dot that appears and disappears among the boulders, till the moment when the sea sweeps into the narrow strait. He comes and goes, follows the rising of the water, amid the flight and cry of the gulls, till the moment when the water's turbulence comes to lick the steps on which the man still sits without moving.

Several weeks earlier, perhaps, the man would have said to the child, "What is your name? How old are you? What do your parents do?" We keep repeating names which have almost no meaning, to hide from ourselves the truth about people, and a person's age is a lie. This was a child who existed for no one, as near and as distant as the wind, as the sea, unpredictable. Besides, the man would have said nothing, for he had not seen the child till the day when, having put on the worn clothes of a fisherman, he had stopped seeing the world through the panes of the window, had moved out onto the terrace, and then sat on the second step of the stone stairs. Unless perhaps the child had been born from his soul.

The child came up, stopped a second, looked at the house, at the man.

"Is it alive?" he wondered.

The man was like a rock, a grey stone statue. Be indifferent, the man thought, let him be. Kindness is often nothing but a yawn of boredom.

"Is it alive?"

Yes, the statue was alive. Even at that time the man's eyes looked out at the world with friendship; his old heart raced in that imperturbable body, the gulls soared into his gaze, the storied ships of the high sea sailed in his blood. The child could not know that. He who loves nature and her pageants is already exiled, a foreigner: from the moment he grows excited, he stands apart, takes his leave. The child was part of nature, marvelously indifferent to the world. The man undoubtedly knew nothing of it either—or is it only later that he fell into that unity which the world cannot tolerate?

No way of knowing, even supposing one could question him. He who escapes division has nothing more to say. If you want to account for an unutterable experience, there's only one possibility: lose yourself in a deep recess, change the cycle of day-to-day boredom into resurrection, turn yourself against the real, don't hold back the melody that swells the silence, let the images unfold. Wait, suffer the void, continue to wait, busy yourself with trifles, with writing, tracing and retracing the outside world, drying it, scraping it with a wire brush until it allows something to show through—something, you can't say what, that was just underneath. Weep at not knowing how to speak, and just as you lose heart, hear the fugitive music that no one else will hear, and wound yourself on a thought that is more true than real, which will never wound those who live on the surface of things.

Perhaps the martin had been wounded so that the meeting could take place. The day came when the child, who had sprung out from among the boulders, caught up in his own excitement, dashed toward the man: he held a bird in his hands.
"Swallow," said the child.
"Martin," said the man.
"Will he fly again?" asked the child.
The martin had a broken wing. They had fussed all morning. They had built a tiny cage. The martin should not be allowed to

move about. With adhesive tape they had clamped the wings to the fragile body, the good one and the sick one. He shouldn't be touched for several weeks.

"Why are his feet so little?" said the child. "If he falls to the ground, is it true that he can never again fly away? Why did God give him such little feet, and such long wings?"

"God!" the man said. "God has no answers. He asks the questions."

The child came with the painted box containing the insects and put it on the second step—because Doña Paca, the housekeeper, would not stand for the child's entering the villa—went off again to his games, came back with the sea.

"You think he'll fly?" the child said one day.

"Patience," the man said.

"They say there are martins here," the child said.

"No, there are only gulls. Here there is too much stone and sun for birds of the open sky."

"How will he know which way to go?"

"He'll know," said the man. "They have their way in their wings, prepared in advance, along with their happiness."

"It's like the rockets," the child said.

"Like the rockets," the man said.

The child had already disappeared. The red-and-black spot hovered a long time over the sea.

But it was only much later, perhaps, that the man saw the sea, the child, the gulls, and the sailing ships on the high seas.

2

*I*n the days after he settled into his new residence—his last, prior to that cramped dwelling from which only trumpets will snatch us—Ramon Rimaz discovered something. The pecking of the typewriters, the constant hum of the office, the ringing of the telephone, the visits . . . he missed them. The murmur of a palace, of which he considered himself the heart, which existed solely because of him, the deferential or timorous faces, the upward gazes that converged on his person, the very luxury that surrounded him, the red hangings, the heavy upholstery, all this used to remind him at every moment that he was needed. It gave him buoyancy, self-confidence, and courage.

The modern, almost elegant white villa seemed to reek of death, as though hundreds of old men, upon their departure, had left behind their breath, their sloth, their weariness. Enormous wardrobes with grooved cornices, potbellied chests of drawers, a red-cushioned prie-dieu, elaborately wrought tables of black wood: this baroque and rococo served to discourage hope. On cupboard ledges and mantelpieces, nothing but pious statuettes dressed like dolls, glass-covered clocks, candelabra, knickknacks, baubles—all the useless things that old shriveled hands had dragged into "this death house," as Campos called it, like so many stillborn sentiments, words abandoned by the spirit, prejudices, the debris of memory.

Doña Paca dusts every day, polishes every Friday. To no end: the dust is encrusted forever in the iron fittings of the wardrobes, in the faded gilding, the tablecloths, the wilted napkins, the stained curtains, the dried boxwood behind each crucifix, in the grooves of the frames of every portrait, on the walls of the drawing room, and along the corridors.

The eyes of the portraits never leave him. They all say: "Let yourself go, Ramon; soon you will be among us." Some seem pious: they are the tall ones, their hands are joined, their eyes fixed in contemplation. They had the gall to pose like that before the camera or for the painter. Naive liars! Others are round: their jovial smile proclaimed the satisfaction of success. They were more true to life. Others, finally, look imperious; decorated and impenetrable, they are constantly dwelling on the same idea: "In my very being I am different than you, I will never confess." But all said: "Ramon, Let yourself go. You're almost there; don't tamper any further with your own image."

In the confined atmosphere of this house-to-die-in, in this bare, stony landscape, treeless, and almost mineral, which can suck up your soul the way the earth drinks blood, Ramon Rimaz thought at first that his life was over. Words like *acceptance, resignation,* and *abandon* rose to his lips. He tried to nourish his spirit on them. But neither the mass that he said every morning in his oratory nor the psalms of the breviary seemed to bring him relief. Sadness and depression made him walk from room to room, mount and descend stairs, and finally sit down in the shade of the patio, his back turned to the sea.

"They're like everyone else," Doña Paca said. The poor man needed his crutches. He never leaves the house. He hides as though he were ashamed.

Doña Paca knew in which wardrobe to look for the burial sheets, the candles, the holy water for the dying.

To have spoken all his life of an eternal life, to have ordained thousands of priests to announce it, to hold in his hands each morning the . . . and now to stand there dry as a stick.

"Unbelievable. Everything happened outside me, I was on exhibit."

No ambition whatever, no future to hope for; he was seated on his tomb. They couldn't take anything more away from him—that was a consolation. But he felt the bitterness that this wisdom veiled. In reality, the evidence was there: he had always lived on plans, hopes—pass examinations, get appointed here, there. Bishop—no, he had never seriously wanted to be a bishop. But scarcely had he become one when he already wanted to be archbishop. As archbishop, he had spent his time worrying about difficulties with the *presidente*, with the *gobernador*, with Rome, hoping that everything would work out, maneuvering with that in mind, and hoping for the cardinal's hat that would free him at last, so he imagined, till the day when, forced by necessity, he had wanted retirement, this house. Hopes, he had always had hopes: but not hope. A formula had come to his lips: the dead end of hope. His house was hope's dead end.

"So the movement that directed my life was external to me"—such was the discovery Ramon Rimaz made. He could have sought out some distractions. Everyday wisdom encouraged him to do so: an entire life spent in the proclamation of the truth, of love and hope, you believe it all sincerely; it was perhaps better not to know that you did not live it. While waiting, it was enough to keep busy, to go from conferences to banquets, to act as if, hoping that others . . . Were the others the same way, believing in everything, capable of dying to protect a truth of which they had no real experience?

For countless invitations came to him from all over—to show himself, to preside, to inaugurate, to give speeches. An unharnessed cardinal is better than no cardinal at all. Silver and golden wedding anniversaries, jubilees, centennials, graduations; civic, religious, and military decorations. It was dizzying to realize how many men there were who seemed to exist only in the empty time of the social comedy.

Diversion seemed to him a trap. His first act of courage was to reject it all. He resolved to stay within himself. Everything began perhaps with that refusal. Still, he did not glory in it. He understood that there was also vanity mixed in with his renunciation. He who had always considered himself an unshakable rock was humiliated because he was no longer self-sufficient and was experiencing boredom. But he also knew that to be nothing but a flowerpot at a ceremony, now that only the insignia of office was left to him and all real power had been withdrawn, was much more humiliating.

Ramon Rimaz, archbishop, cardinal of the Church of Rome, had hesitated a long time. The nuncio, acting by himself, had obtained nothing. Two years before, during a reception at the archbishop's palace—it must have been the time when they presented him with the Cross of Santiago; perhaps they had given it to him simply as a hint that he should step aside—the nuncio, during the banquet, whether acting on orders or speaking for the government or diocesan opinion, had repeatedly commiserated, in a good-natured tone, with the lot of bishops, burdened with such heavy duties in this day and age; he had insinuated that young men . . . After the diplomat had left, Ramon Rimaz, standing erect in the center of the salon, surrounded by his close aides, had proclaimed for all to hear: "The nuncio is getting old." And when they questioned him, he had answered, "Didn't you notice that he repeated the same thing three times?"

Nevertheless, when he learned that he wouldn't have to spend his retirement in Rome, and that he could install himself in a villa that the diocese would place at his disposal, he hesitated no longer. His courage, it seemed, had been fortified by the prospect of having a coadjutor bishop, whom he was in danger of having forced on him sooner or later. And then, as often happens, the decision was precipitated by an insignificant event that Juan Ramon was later to relate to his niece Merché.

It was visiting hour. The last visitor, when he left the room, must have left ajar the leather tambour that was in front of the door to the salon. Juan Ramon, once the visitor was gone and before having the next one brought in, had given himself three minutes to catch his breath. Just as he was about to put his hand on the doorknob he heard a voice that he knew well, a hushed voice that was saying, "He's slowing down, don't you think?" Another, unknown voice had answered, but the words were drowned out in muffled laughter. Nevertheless, he thought he could make out, "Difficult, truly difficult." Ramon had returned to his desk, picked up the telephone, and informed the receptionist that he wouldn't be seeing anyone else. That very evening he had composed his letter of resignation.

"You know," Merché said later, "he spoke of it as if it were something that had happened to someone else, in some remote time."

"Poisoned, I'm poisoned," thought Juan Ramon. "Unbelievable. I would never have known it if I hadn't let go."

In this stagnant period, at this moment when unhappiness seems so total, the desert so endless that you even forget the memory of a moment of peace and plenitude and can't even imagine the slightest relief, Ramon had a sudden start. It was not his will that provoked it but his mirror. Thinking that he'd noticed thickening below his jaws, he took fright, used his eye and hand to check whether his soutane still fell straight and if any sign of obesity was beginning to show, and then laughed at his fear—for to whom, to what could it matter whether he was fat or lean?—and set off. Life is like that; it takes a thousand detours.

So for a time people had been able to watch the tall silhouette stand outlined above the promontory that separates the cove from the village of Noria; and to see him descend the winding path, cross the vacant lot, and advance between the rows of trees. Barely human, these pines, almost plastic—whereas the poplars of the North, how their leaves trembled in the wind! But in those days, no doubt, the images of the world passed across his face as though across stone, and didn't reach his heart.

10

Neither happy nor sad. Profoundly attentive to you-know-not-what, something interior perhaps, or something outside, far off, within as though it were without, without as though it were within. Without a glance to the right or the left, all locked up inside himself so as to smother some cry or other; tall, almost metallic, with a face of bronze. Maybe he was just awfully tired. Or perhaps he was already more awake than is convenient.

All that's needed is an idea, the movement, the seething that precedes an idea; one idea is enough if it gets hold of you, the smallest, tiniest idea that slyly sinks its roots in you, the seed of an idea that begins to germinate—the seed calls for water, humus, air, and fire, and delivers them from their humiliated condition, destroys them in order to exalt them, summons them to the feast of hope. Similarly, the idea, without a face or a name, begins to stir up something in us without our knowledge, it upsets and disorganizes us so as to put one-doesn't-know-what in order, it wounds us, this nuptial idea that leads to a dangerous rebirth. You'd wish your heart were made of stone.

No doubt the glances of others would have been enough to alert him. Rivet your eyes to the ground or lift your head to direct your glance far above everything, like the blind—try as you may, their sharp looks catch you in their net, thicken the air, mire you in shame. Ramon was ashamed to be ashamed. But the fatigue caused by this absurd combat led him back to the house on the cove.

Besides, what need was there for this red cincture, the red buttonholes, the braid that fringed his black soutane? "I'm primping like an old flirt." For two days Doña Paca worked to efface the bright colors. Fearing that the round hat with the shiny fur would still call attention to him, he went out bareheaded. The housekeeper always watched at the window: a cat couldn't enter or leave without her knowing it. Surprised, at first she froze, but a moment later she hurried out brandishing his cardinal's hat— "Your Eminence, Your Eminence!" The saintly woman then witnessed an unbelievable act: Ramon Rimaz turning in a single motion and making a gesture of pushing away, as one repulses a dog, and shouting, "Go on, go on home, silly woman, *tonta mujer!*" Then, with his outstretched arm, he had made, she said, "an obscene gesture," opening and closing his hand twice above the thumb: "Shut up!" She still had tears in her eyes when she thought about it.

The archbishop was submerged in a sort of childhood, as if he were playing a joke on someone. A smile crossed his face. His stride became more brisk. Was he thinking of the annual admonitions that he used to address to his priests on the subject of the biretta or other details of clerical dress? Or did the word come to his lips that Merché, José-Maria, and Doña Paca were to hear so often later on: *Futilidad, futilidad?*

But scarcely had he left the footpath that descended in zigzags on Noria, and crossed the vacant lot that was now given over to scrap iron, garbage, dogs, and the games of the town's poor children, when once again, as he walked through the trees, the stares of everyone were on him. All those faces, the glances of passersby, of the poor, of the old men sitting in front of the hovels that still remained among the white villas, were like a swarm of flies. Their glances stuck to his skin like flies fixed to the sick eyes of an animal, to the milky lips of abandoned nurslings. "I'm making it up; I'm imagining nonsense. Senile psychosis, that's what it must be. Senile psychosis."

His reaction was immediate: instead of applying his mind to avoid their glances, he concentrated on staring them down and put on his ceremonial mask. Most of them yielded. Walk like a king, harden yourself, make yourself implacable; you hardly feel anything now, the blows scarcely graze you. But this was absurd; he wasn't going to wear himself out staring people down. Just look at everything without trying to impose yourself, observe things with the eyes of a superior, slightly disdainful tourist, be blasé. He slowed his pace. He began to relax his gaze. It was simple, he had the technique; all that was needed was to make individuals withdraw into generalizations, to see them *en bloc,* like a river—a pitiful mixture drifting toward death. In this way he imagined he saw humble stares that expected nothing, the flabby glances of the sentimental. Above all, their gaze was weary; they seemed to be begging for some unknown coolness. And the supplicating, almost adoring stares of women—the ones who got down on their knees and tried to kiss his hand. He would make a vague gesture that could as well be one of withdrawal as of benediction. Servile glances that begged more unmistakably than outstretched hands. "Why are you looking at me as though I were God?" But there were also others: some as suspicious as young bulls, looked at him as if they wanted to get away. They said: "Another one, you never stop bumping into priests and soldiers in this country." Glances that crossed over to the opposite sidewalk. And there were others who were open enemies—their stares bore into your eyes; or else, hard and closed, gave you the look one reserves for cops that have given you the third degree. Brutally, a certitude pierced through him: he wasn't imagining this. A reality was revealing itself to him that made his eyes blink.

This is what you get for not staying among your own kind. When he was among his own, surrounded by his priests, by his faithful, or during a ceremony, he felt himself lifted up by their respect, and a sweet warmth, a subtle alcohol, permeated him: at such a moment he could say almost anything with authority. Or he would be smiling, making his way through a crowd, placing his hand on the forehead of a child in its mother's arms, and with amused light irony allowing its lips to touch his ring—he became a being filled with goodness. Had he not even gone sometimes so far as to believe that God visited him then, giving him this mellowed soul? "It's no longer I who live: it is . . ."

"It was the crowd that lived in me. I existed only through their taste for spectacle, which was mixed up with their faith—such meager faith."

Suppose the Son of man had been dressed as the Son of God, recognizable, immediately identifiable, bearing on his person the insignia and the decorations—truly, he would have been misunderstood, for he would have betrayed himself, he would have been marked out too soon, on the basis of appearances: it was necessary that all should be able to hear the sound of a human voice, to see his works, so as to choose in their own hearts. When he wasn't escaping into the hills, he used to get lost in the crowds. Only once had he put it on, his garment of glory; he'd saved it for his three best friends. After the resurrection, Mary had taken him for the gardener; the apostles along the lake thought he was a fisherman. Perhaps it was certitude that tore him apart.

In the time of his glory, Ramon Rimaz had not really thought for one instant of the indifference and hostility of other crowds, beyond the narrow fringe of the devout. They were just the mass of anticlericals, unbelievers, Communists, poor sinners; we should pray for them, try to convince them by improving our methods of communication, and prevent them from doing harm by using the prestige and social power that Providence . . . It was an abstract world. In the same way he, Ramon, had been for them nothing but an abstract being, the representative of an immense organization that impressed some and irritated others, the lieutenant of a despot who wishes to rule over kneeling men. Suddenly, the veneration on which he had been nourished awakened in him a mute anguish, for it had annexed him, turned him into a banner, just as the indiscreet devotion of the crowds substituted a doll made by human hands for the Eternal One, preferred something that would grant victories and dictate the law. All those others, outsiders, he was on their side, too. But how would he get through the passageway? "Have I the right to say that I bring liberation? They can remember; they'd laugh in my face."

These three phrases, he had written them. But when? Impossible to date anything in the notebook that Merché found. It didn't matter.

14

Still, it was more likely that Ramon Rimaz's thinking was not clear in those days. You think, you speak, the way you cry. The way a child cries when she is hungry. Thought is born of fear. You raise the dam of words in order to get rid of your anxiety, to recover a provisional equilibrium. If he had been experienced at this game, Ramon Rimaz would have said to himself, "I am a symbol; it's my cross. What does it matter what I feel? The bets have been placed. One can only hope that, later on, certain reforms will be made." Had he thought in this way with clarity, had he been more versed in such analysis, more accustomed to twist truths for his own convenience and tranquility, he would have been saved. Or lost. Nothing would have happened. But this experience was such a novelty, he'd lived so long outside himself, in hibernation, so to speak, that it disarmed him. Thoughts stirred within him only in their germinal stage, inchoate, stammering, and provoked only a dull uneasiness or naive impulses that left him infinitely astonished.

That is why, after making another half circuit, he resumed his stare, stiffened his face—pull back your shoulders, make yourself a heart of stone—and felt encouraged, not by a thought but a warm surge within him, outside him, a terrible nostalgia. Friendship, the greeting of a man who comes forward, who expects nothing, who has nothing to sell, to give or receive, is neither better nor worse; he steps forward, raises his arms, his countenance becomes open, he looks directly into your eyes: "Hello." Splendid, he doesn't wish you good or evil; he simply exists. Ramon would have liked to raise his hand in greeting.

Just as he was going to leave the narrow pathway and come back to the empty field, a woman ran up, put her knee to the ground, and lifted her face up to him—a tortured face with prominent cheekbones and eyes so blue he could feel them burn. What language was she speaking with that harsh accent? She made a gesture to the fortress. Ramon did not understand—only much later was he to understand—and he traced a vague blessing in the air. The woman grabbed his hand with such passion that anger knotted the cardinal's throat. Something inside him bristled; his own voice frightened him; he didn't recognize it. "Get up; I'm only a man. Does a Christian kneel before anyone? Aren't you ashamed?"

At that she put both knees to the ground and kissed his feet. Ramon stepped away so quickly and with such violence that the woman hesitated but remained on her knees in the dust for a long moment, her hands joined. It was Minka. Their paths will meet again one day along the sea. When the time will have come.

The archbishop decided then to stay indoors. He was drying up with boredom; he tired himself out with doing nothing. He made up his mind to do nothing and to bore himself by his own pure will, and immediately he felt better. Just as, in the depths of agony, when damnation is so complete you no longer can remember a single moment of sweetness and relief is unimaginable, at the instant that, your back to the wall, you become aware of the inevitability of an impossible situation, it sometimes happens that unknown forces rise up and images unfold like chrysalids; so, at the moment when Ramon Rimaz was still saying, "What does it matter that I have been, and am, buried alive? Old body, old heart, passerby, it's all over for you," while he was reciting the psalm that begins. "Out of the depths have I cried to you," and feeling sorry for himself, a few ironic, almost cheerful thoughts caught him by surprise.

At that point the silence of the cardinal filled the house. Previously there was only an emptiness; the silence grows larger with all the words that had been held back, that had been building up.

3

It must have been then, in an apparently dead time, that he had spent hours in front of the potbellied chest of drawers in the drawing room, sorting through the images of his life that Doña Paca had piously stacked in the bottom drawer with the decorations, newspaper clippings, and other proofs of her master's glory. How are we to imagine the cardinal's thoughts before this debris of recollections lying in a drawer? The only thing that is certain is the trenchant order he gave his housekeeper one evening just before supper. This brutal order, along with several things he confided later to Merché, must have a meaning.

Here are some very old photographs, probably daguerreotypes: Ramon must have been in one or more of them, among those dressed-up children, a rosary around his wrist, a book in his hand. Each group was presided over by the same plump matron who stood in the center of the front row, to the right of the priest. This huge woman, a sort of Valkyrie on the wane, with her sunken eyes, her necklaces wrapped around her neck, her hands open and pressed against enormous breasts to show off the diamonds, solitaires, and rings on her pudgy fingers—this was Doña Julia. Julia had a mania: she wanted to be godmother to all the children in the village. She paid for the candles, the rosaries, the missals. All the irrigated land belonged to her. Merché had heard a great deal about her from her family. It was Julia who, on her own authority, took charge of Ramon's education, first at the seminary and then at Rome. But she had died before having the satisfaction of seeing him firmly in the saddle.

Other piles of photographs: engagements, baptisms, graduations, promotions, and among them, in the greatest disorder—because Ramon had wreaked havoc with Doña Paca's organization by plucking out the pink ribbons, which now lay strewn in the dust—photos were scattered about as though his face were in a thousand pieces, images of the glory of Ramon Rimaz, priest, bishop, archbishop, and cardinal, now seated, relaxed and smiling, as if to say, "See how humble I am, how I enjoy myself like everyone else"; now standing, grave, wearing his look of authority, alone or surrounded by his aides; now kneeling, his hands firmly joined at the prie-dieu, his eyes lifted to heaven, raised in ecstasy. You were lying, Ramon, you were lying and you didn't know it. And there were pictures of him with important people, between the *gobernador* and the *alcade,* dominating them because of his height, proud or humiliated to be exposing himself this way at election rallies, fairs, or celebrations of false, long-ago victories, perhaps indifferent, simply waiting for it to be over.

All these faded, incoherent photos, all mixed up, undated, no longer with any sentimental tie to hold them together: they were a declaration of something. A banal something, which we all believe we've felt at least once, that pointless, sentimental nostalgia which makes the heart liquid for a second: but sometimes it can pierce you by surprise, beyond regret or pity, to the soul's very marrow. These photos of everyone, which end up relegated to attics where they lie abandoned along with once-winged love letters: love has left them, the lovers have disappeared, their faces are scattered in dusty heaps. Fools, why did you want to put your past in a box, why eternalize the moment, why look at Medusa, fetishists? Couldn't you live in the streaming joy of death? One sees men standing there, strutting young roosters who wanted to get themselves shot for someone, for themselves, who stick out their chests: they have borrowed a fancy uniform or a dress suit.

One hand rests negligently on a console, the other is perhaps stroking their moustache. Then there are those society ladies or their housemaids, who have put on the robes of a duchess for five minutes. These indecent pictures— but who recognizes that they are indecent?—of first communions, which try to proclaim for all time what has perhaps never been and what will never be again; or those shameless wedding pictures, those newlyweds, associates in fantasy, exposed to the sighing crowd that pretends to believe in the marvelous and naively invents false memories of sentiments they never experienced. How we love to use up in spectacle, in celebrations, in one day, the secret that should lift up an entire life!

The child, in any case, had been to communion long before; on that day, he was trying to mimic the feelings he had been told he should have, and which no one ever felt, which perhaps, to his desperation, he didn't feel at all, or which he would quickly cease to feel, and then come to believe that he was moving away from a God he'd never met except in borrowed sentiments. As for the girl smothered in frothy white and the boy disguised as a headwaiter, perhaps they haven't waited for this day, and in any event night would bring no revelation to them. What did it matter? All had passed through the same door. The actors and the spectators were now dispersed to the four winds, were in the process of rotting, or had already become dust, returned to the carbon circuit, were decomposing into memory. They were barely a name on a genealogical tree on a tombstone, or perhaps on the door of one of those stacked burial compartments, the low-rent buildings of death in our big cities today—already dead before death, in the very instant the camera clicked—or on those faded photos that had captured them in the prime of their youth. There they were, their hearts swollen with desires, their heads bursting with projects, surrounded, they believed, by the warm admiration of all, already set in their ways, petrified in borrowed clothes—and viewed from this distance, all clothes were borrowed; the flesh itself was borrowed: the society woman and the

19

housemaid seem cruelly to converge—all these faces that eyes once contemplated, that caused hearts to beat faster, which to someone were more necessary than bread, all acknowledged the same thing, as though time were the only revealer.

Just like those newsreels of thirty or forty years ago, in which solemn dignitaries, heroes to their contemporaries, declare, declaim, inaugurate, congratulate, call to war or to peace, decorate or are decorated, bury or are buried, all spectacles watched by solemn crowds that were moved to emotion; in which the officers of long-past wars, already recognized as futile, extend an arm or brandish a sword, and soldiers rush about, bounding like rabbits, the heroes who flee forward, the cowards caught up in the process, all snatched up by a movement that is not theirs. These are the great of this world with their top hats, their eternal smile for the cameras, the war leaders, the soldiers, the cowards, and the brave, and those who are neither cowardly nor brave, carried away by a movement that is not in them, rich and poor jumbled together, those who watch and those who are watched, applaud or are applauded, puppets on the stage for an instant, whose ideas and feelings no longer have any importance and perhaps never did have, pure reflections of anonymous forces born outside of the liberty of consciousness. All find themselves jumbled together in the same general contempt, at least for a few seconds, till the public recovers its historic and slightly condescending gravity, the several seconds needed for the eye to adjust and lend itself to the unaccustomed rhythm of sixteen images per second, while laughter spreads through the house at this stiff running, these jerky gestures, these mouths that open immoderately but emit no sound, as if time were the only revealer, forcing us to recognize the emptiness of speeches, the fakery of battles, the enormous uselessness of social ceremonies, however necessary. As long as the Prince of this world keeps his power and plays with the ambitions and vanities that build careers equally well on truth as on falsehood, as long as he succeeds in convincing us that what is cannot be otherwise, so that men and women allow themselves to be destroyed by the social virtues as well as by vices, drawn on by movements not their own, phantoms of truth that have become hard as stones because they have not first been lived interiorly but have been seized upon in the vertigo of propaganda and power, all of us, no longer even aware that we have deserted a soul that we arrogantly wear on the outside like a badge on a lapel, will confuse it with those ideas that reign for a season before perishing in universal esteem. As if time were the only revealer.

And someone, should the angel of solitude come to select and compel him to live from then on with that in him which cannot be named, this interior awareness that makes him follow the passing parade through reversed binoculars, how could he not know the stupor, or the frenzy to which dance gives birth, or the irrepressible laughter of the child at the puppets that flop about on the miniature stage, pulled by invisible strings? Unless, by some grace, divine compassion should come to subdue mockery, curing the ironic complacency of one who, thinking himself different, masks his envy beneath bitterness, and unless the *misereor super turbam* resounds over this perishable and baptized flesh, which, in its shifting diversions as well as its imperturbable gravity, proclaims its innate poverty.

In this way infinite space had perhaps already opened in the full silence of Ramon Rimaz's house, but slyly and as though without his knowledge. Only fools could possibly think that he yielded to contempt and was prey to despair; or simple souls who think that everything is ruined when appearances collapse. Beyond your social arrangements and compromises, a joy can spring up, my friends, that you will perhaps never have the slightest notion of. And doubtless it was another unreasoned, secretly joyful impulse that made him say one evening, in a hard voice, while pointing to the bottom drawer, "Burn. *Quema. Quema.*"

The old woman's piety had not been able really to accept this sacrifice. The relics had been transferred to the attic; that is how, with Merché's complicity, I was able to turn them over and over in my hands, as he had done, the images of the glory of Ramon Rimaz, apostle, who for forty years, his face impenetrable, had remained in harness, had been part of the feast-day programs along with presidents, governors, deans, consuls, and all the notables who do their duty while spoiling their nature. They exhaust their universal love in long speeches and patiently shed their courage, leaf by leaf, scheming, tracking down schemes, deceiving people for their own good, consoling the poor, reassuring the rich, keeping their heads above the current, weeping over catastrophes, celebrating victories.

All the newspaper clippings, illustrated by photos, exalted the character, the virtue, the piety, the prudence, and the humility of the archbishop. These clippings, whose vocabulary was curiously limited, were all alike—not a shadow of fantasy in them, no humor whatever. Such journalism seemed dedicated to ceremony. Whatever was alien to the devout language of justification or adulation seemed unknown to it: as if all the articles had been prepared in advance by some office and all there was left to do was to fill in the blank spaces with names and the date.

Martinez Campos used to tell a story about something that happened to the new archbishop, Ramon's successor; it was still recent enough to amuse him. The new archbishop was to preside over a ceremony in honor of Saint Teresa of Avila and give a speech. At the last minute, a bad cold kept him at home. Nevertheless, the next day's papers had not only described the ceremony but summarized and commented on the admirable speech. Campos, who seemed acquainted with the French press, said: "What we need is a Christian satiric newspaper, a *Canard enchaîné* for believers, something that would wake us from our false seriousness and spiritual childishness."

One of the clippings I saw later contained an interview with Ramon Rimaz, future cardinal, on his departure for Rome. It provided details on the number of trunks and suitcases he was taking along, the red and violet stockings, and the other accessories in each color—after all, though he would return as a cardinal, he was leaving as a bishop—the buckled slippers, the sandals; then came the list of the seventeen items that made up the wardrobe of a prince of the Church. Did poor people read this kind of junk?

And yet, while I was rummaging through the old photographs of the cardinal's past glory as if some secret might be hidden in them that would throw some light on the strange outcome of this story, someone warned me against any hasty interpretation. Resentment because of what he had been and was no longer, or else a desire to escape complacency, could of course explain the order he addressed to Doña Paca, but there could be no question of a denial of his past.

Once more I thought I heard the frail voice of Martinez Campos as he lay stretched out on his chaise lounge while, his diaphanous hands above his face, in the light from the bay—his face was in shadow, his hands in the light—he tried to pinpoint some difficult truth or other. After the events that occurred, I had gone several times to the archbishop's palace to see Campos, who had been Ramon's secretary, in an effort to understand. Campos would pass without transition from humor to lyricism as though his skepticism were merely the other side of a burning certitude. His language was friendly and devoid of verneration. He had accompanied his patron to Rome five times, he told me; he had lived for years close beside him. He had thought he understood. He weighed him, judged him, sized him up: he had been wrong. Because now that everything had been acted out, now that Ramon had done this admirable and foolish thing, performed this act, perhaps the last of his life, it all took on a different light. A life could be illuminated by a single act at its close, he said, a single act that changed the meaning of all the rest. "It's a good kick in the behind," Martinez said, "for all us bookkeepers, copyists, and notaries."

But to hear him talk, if Ramon by some impossibility were to govern again, to be in the same situation, he would behave exactly as before—drab in his speeches and administration, impenetrable during ceremonies; no doubt he had a clear awareness of what his role called for.

Campos himself made the same distinction between ritual and religious show as between speech and publicity. Parades, publicity, all the forms of propaganda and spectacle—he'd give them away to the devil if the devil would take them. But, he continued, the gospel couldn't be delivered to the world in its pure essence. If the soul were without a body, there would no longer be a soul. A love without some degree of opaqueness would no longer be a tangible love. The Church had constructed its body, the body that was its shell, which had grown larger century by century. The fire was not blazing up because the walls were too high, the shell too thick. But perhaps the fire should not be allowed to burn with too high or bright a flame. Otherwise the crowds would come, fascinated like flies around a lamp; they would clap their hands, be overly receptive to miracles but blind to the heart of things, wanting the resurrection, of course, but certainly not the agony or the death. The Church, with its ramparts, its possessions, its works of art, the Vatican, the cardinals—none of all that existed for itself but rather so as to permit a revelation in human consciousness. Certainly the means might mask the end. In any case, it was necessary to pass through scandal and overcome the obstacles. But total purity would be a yet greater obstacle. Had I read Nietzsche? "Everything profound moves forward in disguise." Did I understand? Once he got started, Campos hardly cared whether or not you answered.

Had I ever been in Rome for the Easter vigil? The new fire was lit there that night, ahead of all the other churches of Rome and the world, and all who wanted to could go forth with their own light deep within them. What did all the display of baroque matter, all the imperial phantasmagoria, the heavy layers of custom, these cardinals, bishops, prelates, and canons who advanced in the procession, fat, skinny, young or old, functionaries with parched hearts, skeptics or mystics, lukewarm, pietistic or pious, every one of them decked out in fancy uniforms, bundled up in capes, chasubles, and dalmatics! They had no name. Scarcely a face. They advanced masked, absorbed by the symbols; they offered the fire like the bread, the wine, and the oil, as sacrament and mystery. "They'll organize a banquet to celebrate all that"—Campos had a horror of ecclesiastical banquets—"where, in compensation for the fatigue and rarely acknowledged boredom caused by ceremonies that go on forever, they'll tell one another stupid stories about promotions." It didn't matter. The world was what it was; each could be faithful to his or her part of the light.

Sheltered behind her walls, the Church might well play the official games; she maintained a diplomatic corps that seemed to be staffed primarily by those who had faith only in the visible body; she paraded her ridiculous Swiss guards; she supported men's weakness by flattering their vanity, by distributing costumes, collars, sashes, ribbons, crosses—"the order of Christ," Campos said, "have you heard of it? They award it to heads of state. Isn't that wild?" She allowed factions to develop in her cramped fortress, conspiracies among all those who, ingenuously, linked their destinies to God's. "That scandal-mongering novelist of yours—what's his name? Has the style of an aristocrat and the soul of a concierge, to say the least, like those insects that lay their eggs in carrion and then eat them. For the rest, I've nothing against him. . . . The sewers of a huge city, they're truly amazing—but they aren't the city. Everybody knows there's more to Rome than Fra Angelico. That apologist of yours wants to argue that the sewers bear witness to the city. Long live—what's his name?"

And Saint Peter's in Rome, had I been there? "That was quite an idea of Bernini's, to set saints on the columns of the piazza. The Church might have placed scholars or artists there, but that would have been a display of vanity. Or her worst enemies, whom she had nourished, who turn against her while brandishing the truths with which she has sown the flesh of the world—she might stick them up on the quadruple colonnade among the hundred and forty saints, like witnesses of the fire. What do you say to that?"

Martinez Campos raved on in that style. Two red spots on the cheekbones of his pale, bony face constituted an alarm signal. His hands ceased to stir the light; he crossed them on his chest, closed his eyes for a moment, and was silent as though stopped by some image. Coming to a standstill again, perhaps at Saint Peter's Square after so many rainy days had passed, he got started once more: "No doubt but Ramon was aware of all these things; nevertheless, I believe I may say . . .

"One morning," he continued in a much lower voice, while his hands remained still and he kept his eyes closed a long time, "one morning we had just left the courtyard of Saint Damasus, we'd turned under the colonnade for a bit of cool air and were crossing the piazza for the last time—you know, that freedom that the most secret of men can have, that sincerity one feels on the last day of a vacation or at the end of a trip, with your business completed and the return ticket in your pocket, just as you're about to put on the harness again, maybe that was it—we were between the colonnade and the obelisk, among the horse cabs. Ramon Rimaz stopped short, looked me in the eye, and lowered his voice: 'I'm going to tell you something, Campos'—addressing me familiarly, perhaps by mistake, as the old professor had addressed him—'I have never crossed this square without . . . I had a professor at the Gregorian.'"

And even while writing this, I could see Ramon, who was a young student then, immobile beside the old professor, listening to the perhaps flagging voice, which was saying: "I have never crossed this square without . . ." Then years later, when Ramon Rimaz was almost old, with his head bent forward and pointing a finger at the basilica: "I have never crossed this square without . . ." And I too remember standing one morning motionless on that same square, years after listening to Campos, with the images of Martinez, Ramon, and the old professor clear in my memory, seeing Saint Peter's, always there—a bird grazing it with its wing for billions of years would scarcely dent it; and that's still not eternity, as my mother used to say when I was a child. Seeing the colonnades and the cabs were still there, I raised my eyes to Maderno's baroque facade and felt oppressed by the enormity and the quantity of it all. Then, without warning, the sun's rays struck that pure, airy cupola, miraculous, light as a dance, as obvious as a smile, and suddenly I was flooded with certainty that the building needed all its mass to take root, to spring up into the light.

Then Ramon Rimaz continued, lowering his voice: "I had a professor at the Gregorian. One morning we were crossing the square, right here, I can still hear his voice as he pointed to Saint Peter's: 'I've been here twenty years now and I've never crossed this square without thinking of Luther. Leo X, wanting to finish the basilica, called in the best artists of Florence and of all Italy. That cost a lot of money. So he sent out an appeal to Christendom. There was a bishop in Mainz, an insatiable Hohenzollern: his two bishoprics weren't enough for him, he coveted a third. Lists of indulgences and their prices were posted on all the churches in Germany. The bishop set aside a sizable percentage for himself. It's at this moment that Luther emerges one morning from the university chapel, sees this poster, and rises up. . . . You know all that better than I, and also what they say: it was the occasion, not the cause.'"

Continuing to walk on, just as the old professor had, Rimaz said: "While one part of Christendom was yielding to angelism and the illusions of conscience, the other was staging spectacles and permitting the build up of a public relations and administrative machine, something almost military." And suddenly he broke out in strong, happy laughter: "Pretty soon the Italians will be the only ones who love opera."

Martinez Campos continued, almost ashamed: "You're going

to think I'm preaching." Then, perhaps because he wanted to lighten the atmosphere by giving his remarks an ironic edge, he laughed like a child, just as we laugh at our own jokes: "Do you know the one about your French bishop, have you heard it? No, I don't know his name; I've no memory at all for surnames. The story has even reached us here. He's driving along in his little Renault. There's a blowout. He gets to work. A society woman passes by: 'Your Excellency! Your Excellency!' she fawns, marveling at His Greatness's simplicity, 'may I kiss your ring?' And negligently pointing at something with the jackhandle, he said, 'In the tool box, dear lady, in the tool box.' I'm sure you've heard that one."

But what aberration had led Ramon Rimaz to allow himself to be embalmed in this syrupy literature? The brochure I had just extracted from the photographic archives and whose pages I was now turning was damning. Had he yielded to an access of insensitivity or vanity, like those once bold and committed writers who were clever enough to make their fortune in the service of truth and, having fallen into the holy water, were listened to by their pious clientele now that they no longer had anything to say? And who, once they'd become honored masters, distinguished doctors, have or permit to be published thick volumes dedicated to their own glory, edited by hangers-on, the future masters and doctors? Or was it merely indifference or lassitude that had made him say, "All right, since they want this kind of drivel!" One hundred and fifty pages, glossy paper, and twenty-four photographs, of which eight were in color. Its author was one Francisco Pizzaro. The latter's picture had its place at the outset near the cardinal's, basking in the glory of his master.

In brief, Ramon was a *great man of God:* he had deserved to be born of a good mother, of a good father, to be priest, bishop, archbishop, and cardinal. His elevation was a *great honor* to the diocese and the nation, a proof of the *particular affection* of the Holy Father.

The presentation of the cardinal's hat was especially fascinating. Twelve distinguished personages under an enormous chandelier: two bishops, several monsignori, a member of the Academy, the ambassador, a Dominican. In the center, Ramon. He was holding the letter of nomination in his right hand; with the left, he was sketching out something that looked like a gesture of rejection—while his open mouth registered amazement or fright. The others, who stood in a semicircle leaning slightly toward the nominee, looked surprised and delighted, with perhaps just a tiny hint of humor or envy in some of the rather forced smiles. But one might also assume that the photographer was responsible, since the surprise that protocol required them to feign (the fact had been known for months) had to be prolonged or repeated in order to have it immortalized on film. At the far right of the semicircle and standing slightly to the rear, the Dominican was having trouble hiding his boredom. The *di calore* visits had lasted three days, and the list of notables present took two pages. But it was the *imposition of the hat,* not to be confused with *the presentation of the hat,* that seemed to be the feature of these festivities. All the Roman aristocracy was on hand, innumerable heads of state, ministers, and ambassadors, who thereby proclaimed to the world their faith in the gospel. It was above all the blare of the trumpets, the vivid colors, that had dazzled Pizzaro; his piety overflowed; he described a night at the opera: "The garnet-red carpet that overflowed the steps of the papal throne, the red hangings of the seats and the galleries," he wrote, "blended marvelously with the green of the carpet, which demarcated the choir. The violet robes of the bishops and prelates, the multicolored habits of the religious, the braided dress coats of the diplomats, the Knights of Malta and of the Holy Sepulchre, of the Privy Chamberlains of Sword and Cape, the officers of the Noble Guards, the Palatine Guards, the sumptuous Swiss Guards, the Papal Gendarmes, and in the crowd the glittering dresses of Rome's great ladies, the sparkle of diamonds, the flame of gold kindled by a deluge of light: it is in this fabulous setting that the imposition of the hat takes place.

Tears come to one's eyes and one feels proud to be a Christian," concludes Pizzaro. And I imagined again the pure cupola struck by the sun, the unbelievable smile.

One chapter was titled, "From Reception to Reception." Nothing but ceremonies and banquets. Ramon made speeches, proposed toasts. His motto was: *Humilidad*. He had spoken on many occasions of humility, "the greatest of the virtues." Undoubtedly, wearied by so many functions, he was trying to hang on to formulas that had served him well every time he had to speak and had nothing to say. *Humilidad*—this was the virtue the modern world needed; this was what needed to be revealed to a world that was trying to make itself God, *humilidad*.

And I saw again Ramon Rimaz sitting before the potbellied chest of drawers, turning the pages of his life, hearing once again his own words in the same way you'd hear those of another, thinking perhaps of the millions of men and women who were starving, sacrificed to principles, tortured in the name of liberty, order, or revolution, even killed, while he, covered with splendor on his pontifical throne, had for years been reciting, over and over, *humilidad*.

Did he have the stomach to read through to the end of this horrible pamphlet, which was now describing the return to the city? The sumptuous parade from the presidential palace to the cathedral, during which he stood in the luxurious open car, the tasseled red hat on his head, smothered and sweating under the purple cape fringed with gold. The final chapter had been consecrated to the reception offered by the *alcade* and the *gobernador*. "The entire *Who's Who* was there," Pizzaro said. They had taken advantage of the occasion to decorate him with the Order of Santiago. The *gobernador* was not one to miss such a fine opportunity: "I salute the unity of Church and state, so marvelously realized in your person; the Church, the army, and the administration united for the prosperity of the fatherland, giving to the world an example of order and peace." And Ramon, who had given the response that had to be given, that religion was the strongest support of society . . . Shout, Ramon, cry out! I tried to imagine him, rising to his full height, swollen with anger, suppressing the words: that Christianity was at the service of no state, of no country, but was first of all at the service of liberty and the salvation of the living.

Was it anger or shame? One thing is certain: an idea had stirred in him, an obscure impulse was rousing him when he shouted to Doña Paca, his voice hard, pointing to the clippings, the brochures, the photos, all the debris of the past: Burn. *Quema.*

4

~~~~~~

*W*hy, that same evening, did Ramon Rimaz, who in those days never left the house on the side facing the sea, come and sit on the second of the stone stairs?

It could have been an evening like this one. The sun, falling behind the islands, sets a splotch of light dancing on a ship's mast beyond the inlet. The light mounts the length of the mast as the sun sinks. How rapidly it mounts! The sea settles; voices along the path are already stilled. Just as the sun teeters, the tiny flag atop the mast bursts into a flame as brief as a kind thought. Why are we so miserly with ourselves? The darkness traces the sierra in pure lines on the blue of the sky, as though with a hand. The red ocher turns to brown, the cypresses of the threshing grounds along the Altata road mount to the sky, and while the night reclines gently on the sea, the village emerges from the earth and comes alight at the same time as the sky. The water carriers, the mine workers, the gypsies who are going up to Altata are already no more than shadows. They are the dead passing by. What do their desires, their loves, their plans, matter? They are only the dead passing. It must have been an evening like this one.

You can watch just about anything with this sort of detachment, sad or happy: a nightfall, for instance, with faceless passersby who come and go, people who have passed by for centuries and centuries—they disappear, others come by with the same desires, the same gestures, walking on these stones that have been worn down by so many steps; spectacles and vague ideas that imprint themselves in us almost without our cooperation—

something like that. You find it all banal, that's what's essential. You pay no attention, you let yourself go, following the shadowed paths that open into the caverns of the great deep. Suddenly the thing is there, exploding, lacerating. An unspeakable panic sweeps everything away—as in the Goya canvas at the Prado in which you see a monster covering the picture while below him a tempest of fear sweeps away the crowd: alone in the foreground, an ass stands motionless and peaceful—it is the thundering intuition of contingency, of the unimportance of everything, a terror without a name, unless perhaps it is the presentiment of some unbelievable joy.

Ramon thinks: is this death? He believed his heart was failing; he let himself slip back against the steps, supporting himself on his two elbows, and closed his eyes. The evidence had been given him that it would suffice, not to will it, but simply to let himself go, to follow the route that had opened into the depths, if he wished to pass to the other shore. But what route? The evening was ordinary enough. As for the chain of ideas and images that had led him to this unheard of vision, he could no longer understand it. As he was standing up very carefully like an invalid, and although he felt no symptom, neither heart flutters nor dizziness, he wondered whether some unknown malaise might not account for such a revelation—the revelation of what? Night had come. Life is like a day. It is time to go home. It must have been then that he had written in his notebook: "Vertigo. I thought for a second that I was master of my life and death."

Hold yourself in a deep recess, cross one by one the infernal circles of sensation, of images, of sentiments, of ordinary ideas, be patient enough to put up with privation: out of that very destitution a man would perhaps be born. But in order not to experience the extreme limit of desert and thirst, the mind bustles about: nothing but objects, projects, chores, changes, pleasures, hopes and fears, heartbeats, a thousand flutters to recover an endlessly elusive balance. Push ahead with hurried steps: it's an escape. Take on altitude: it's a longer drop. Anything that veils the abyss will do. Someone who would stop to contemplate it would perhaps fall like a stone into happiness.

Though Ramon Rimaz wanted with all his heart to get off this road that had led him to the frontier—but how, if it's all unknown to you, and it takes you by surprise?—he persisted in his determination to stand aside rather than put his faith in circumstances; he would pull himself through by sheer will-power. In the meantime, he would avoid the sea at nightfall.

At the archbishop's palace they were worried. If Ramon refused to appear, no longer presided, no longer inaugurated, it was unlikely that this was for reasons of discretion, since the new bishop had many times begged him to come. After all, a cardinal existed only in order to make appearances. Ramon, therefore, must be ill. How could they have known that he was entering into health? If a living dog was worth more than a dead lion, then an unyoked cardinal could still be of use. So they ought to check up on him and perhaps prevent him from falling apart altogether. They sent the vicar-general, Francisco Pizzaro, whom Ramon had promoted just before retiring.

Pizzaro came on a visit of gratitude. Young and svelte: a movement took form at the small of his back, lifted him up, held up his head, and gave him an ardor, a freshness—Pizzaro was destined for a handsome future. He appeared in violet. His violet verged on red. Ramon was dressed in a black soutane. Pizzaro was surprised, whereas Ramon marveled that someone would appear embellished in that way except in a ceremony, but he let nothing show. Nevertheless, Francisco thought he had to offer an excuse: he had just baptized the sixteenth child of a family in a nearby village; he wasn't going to change his clothes and drag along a lot of luggage. It was an explanation. Ramon said he bet Don Jesu Gonzalez had been party to the proceedings. Yes, Gonzalez had been the godfather as usual, Francisco answered.

"But really," continued Ramon, "the human species seemed pretty well stocked; is it quantity . . .?"

Faced with the vicar-general's astonishment, Ramon was start-led to feel a huge laugh building up, which would have shaken him to his toes if he hadn't immediately suppressed it by exaggerating the gravity of his features. Francisco quickly recov-ered. The recent promotion had further developed his self-confidence and gave him that slightly protective and benevolent tone that people take with old men when they themselves are still in the race, naively unaware that such condescension conceals an insult. Francisco talked: so and so had died, so and so was replacing him: "It was time to think of a successor for the dean, who was, really, losing his marbles; yes, according to him every time he went out in the street he met the Holy Father, who explained Vatican policy to him. The poor dean had always had delusions of grandeur, now he was entering his second childhood—can you think of a name? Besides, His Excellency is asking no one's advice; all one has to do is propose a name for him to . . . you see what I'm getting at. Ah, yes, there was also the Christian Labor group, which was causing trouble as usual, fussing over the salaries of church personnel, and bringing out onto the public square things that should remain within the house. They're playing into the hands of the Communists. As for the *gobernador,* no problem there; rumors were circulating, but in the last analysis he had the sense of the Church. The *alcade?* The *alcade* would grant a new lease, no problem. And the diocesan confraternity was becoming a real support."

The cardinal understood that he had set a fashion in one thing at least: "no problem." That was the device he should have inscribed on his arms: "no problem." The vicar-general's voice reached him from far off like familiar music, the phrases almost detached from their meaning. A word began to take shape from deep within him: *mundanalidad,* worldliness. Why had he ap-pointed this fellow? The confraternity backed another candidate, had thought it could impose him: at the last minute he, Ramon, had brandished Pizzaro. The man was merely ambitious, which is to say, insignificant. It sometimes happens that the more medio-cre people are, the more you aid them in advancement; you thereby prove your power, since you're drawing something from the void.

Perhaps a scene had returned to the cardinal's attention: one that took place while driving back in the car after a confirmation, and which Martinez Campos told me about later. Ramon liked to be accompanied by his chancellor, a sort of philosopher outside the mainstream who seemed to have nothing to lose, nothing to gain; he was a stranger to fear, a pious and lucid man, very rare. Ramon, perhaps to reassure himself about his choice, asked: "And our own vicar-general?"

"For me," Campos said, "his principal quality is to have been appointed."

"He has a good character," said Ramon.

"Might it be, then, that he has none?" the chancellor answered, bursting into laughter.

That was what he had always sought: peace, nothing to disturb the surface. He had never before understood this so clearly; and all the while the music continued, Pizzaro's voice became almost friendly and passed on various invitations. He had to answer. It would be absolutely pointless to declare that from now on he wished to refuse unnecessary contacts, futile conversations, the chance circumstances that make decisions for us—that he was weary of these meetings, these banquets where everyone plays at being what he is supposed to be. A phrase forced itself on him: "I'm busy elsewhere." Aside from the fact that as far as he knew he was busy at nothing, what was the point of disturbing Francisco? Only a pious phrase would serve to establish his defense. So he raised his long, withered face and set his gaze straight into the eyes of the vicar-general—saw them for the first time and under the shock closed his own for an instant. Then he said: "My friend, at my age, it is time to be serious and prepare for death." The desired effect was produced. Panic, for a brief second, troubled Pizzaro's tranquil features. He must see a doctor. Promise. He knew an excellent doctor. Ramon Rimaz promised.

The car had scarcely disappeared in the red dust of the road as Ramon reentered the house, opened the door to the drawing room, bumped into the armchairs, and groped his way to the shutters: the light came in, tumultuous as a flight of screaming birds. A moment later he was standing before the mantel with desperate attention, studying his eyes in the wavy glass of the mirror: he thought he saw in them a golden, ironic gleam—and was satisfied.

He had often wondered how certain men, whom he had met at important church functions, could combine such contradictory qualities. On one hand, they had the martial bearing expressed by the imperious gesture and peremptory tone of voice which proclaimed frankness and boldness, and on the other, a certain uneasiness, a readiness to collapse, a frantic need to escape, the minute these thundering warriors found themselves confronted by a thought that didn't seem to fit the situation and threw things off. Of course, this was true only if the thought came from above, for in the mouth of an inferior it could be ignored, treated with scorn, attributed to envy or clumsiness. Nothing even had to be said; disdain could emerge from a simple glance. So in the very instant when he, Ramon, face to face with Pizzaro, was suppressing ideas that would perhaps have been dangerous, and in any event pointless—not without some shame, he started to use what suddenly seemed to him a technique of deception, although he had so often and so naturally used the same procedure in the past. Just as his gaze stabbed into the eyes of his interlocutor, before he modestly lowered his pupils in order to drop a pious thought that, eliminating all discussion, would close the door and permit the one who expressed it to ascend into an inaccessible world—at that very moment, panic had crossed the virile face of the vicar-general.

It was an Etruscan statue that had arisen then before Ramon's eyes, as he saw the face before him for the first time. What was it called? He had never been much for museums. A vague uneasiness, that was all he felt when he passed through the Vatican galleries, an uneasiness never expressed at the time but had been translated then and there by the phrase "What an idea, to lodge the pope in a museum!" But he had often stopped before this bronze warrior—Mars, that was it, the Mars of Todi, a handsome, muscular warrior in bronze, whom at first glance you might mistake for a dancer. Power and suppleness, dash: you felt like throwing out your chest and you walked with a lighter stride. But there was something missing, and it made you shudder. The colored incrustations on the eyes had been torn away, as in Greek statues: Francisco Pizzaro's eyes said the same thing as the dead eyes of the Mars of Todi—the sadness of not existing. Just as the painter mixes certain colors, hot gray with cold gray, to obtain a neutral, so the eyes of the warrior-dancer and the eyes of Pizzaro proclaimed a void. That's how the world operates, Ramon thought: when you were unable or didn't have the courage to exist by yourself, in your own strict truth, then in order to escape the consciousness of your nothingness, the desert of your consciousness, the boredom of your days, you sculpted your own statue. Your gaze lost its humanity, and you tried, with the patience of a mole and agonizing humility, to exist on the outside. You identify yourself with your role to the point that having reached some pedestal, you set yourself up as a master because you were finally able to demonstrate your own importance through the deference shown by others. How solid you became, how little mortal! You guided the world—but first the world created you. And you forgot that. But the eyes were there to acknowledge it.

That's how Ramon was thinking. Or rather, his thoughts formed and decomposed independently within him as he sat on the stone stairs, his hands joined on the ivory knob, in his faded blue clothes, an almost gray statue against the white of the villa. Or was it later? Must have been somewhat later that he asked Doña Paca to buy him old fishing clothes and that he took to walking along the shore. What does it matter?

Ramon had written in his notebook: "Pizzaro has empty eyes like the Mars of Todi." This visit had revealed something to him; and I was able to come upon the images and thoughts that, on some days, hid the sea from him. Not that he took pleasure in evoking them: they set in motion within him an incomprehensible anxiety that forced him to discover that he did not know what it was he knew. He had thought that the gospel encouraged those who mounted the stage to put on an air of modesty and compunction. He himself, at each promotion, had forced himself to experience such feelings. How many times he had found them false in others! Without any doubt, it was a humility that he talked himself into, an oratorical truth that he fooled himself with in order to increase his merit in his own eyes, to be pardoned by others for a too rapid ascent, in order, without too much shame, to invite others to obedience. Of course, he had been perfectly sincere then, but he had remained apart, outside his own experience.

And brusquely a thought surged within him that brought him to his feet and led him in long strides down to the shore—which I follow among the gulls' wings now that he is no longer there, because his thoughts carried him too far. Ramon continued along, accompanied by the rushing of wings, paying no heed to the gulls that now walk, now hop, now fly off in front of him, draw a curve over the sea, land, set themselves in motion again behind him, hop again, almost take off, fall like thoughts that are too heavy, and finally fly off when he turns round and starts back, tracing a new curve in the opposite direction over the cove's nearly perfect oval. The swishing of the wings blends with the crackling of the pebbles as his steps crush out the star-shaped tracks left by the birds, while the sea, churned by the boulders of the gully, erases both their tracks with milky water. But Ramon is unable to pay attention to any of this because a naive thought is penetrating him like a sword: that the gospel does not encourage us to feel sentiments or try to imitate attitudes. Instead, with tranquil authority, it announces a reality: he who agrees to govern would be the last, is in fact the last, because he became, because he is forced to become, a being without compassion, an instrument of social physics, almost necessarily identified with what is inhuman in the world, as interchangeable as a slave. Such an individual has only one chance to pull himself free and escape such a hardening: to enter the path of the gospel by overturning the natural order of things, just as it does—and to appear, not in words and symbols, but as he is in reality—the poorest and the last.

"I was asleep and I didn't know it," murmured Ramon as he walked, and as I now walk, along this very shore, while shame seizes me at overhearing his groan, just as anguish can grab your throat when you make phrases and invent images in order to avoid taking the route to which they beckon.

But as the reader already knows, Ramon Rimaz was neither philosopher nor writer; he had not learned to make use of thought simply for the sake of his own equilibrium. Ideas struck him like blows. Now he is climbing up all the steps of the stone passageway and reenters the villa before the dangerous hours of night.

5

~~~~~~

*C*url up all night like a sick animal, worn out, cut to the bone in an all-powerful wind. For four days it has been whistling through the grove of pines, charging against the boulders with a howl, raising dust on the Altata road, lashing, digging, lifting the frantic sea under a piercingly blue sky, penetrating under doors, infiltrating window cracks, and boring into nerve and bone. Despairing of its useless force, the straining, pent-up wind, tireless as a persistent thought, drives itself to exasperation, calms down, starts up again, swells, exalts, butts endlessly against necessity, turns it, gnaws it, and thinks it is about to destroy it, only to discover new barriers. Roll back and forth in bed. Be unable to sleep or to watch, encourage yourself to hope with naive images, desire to see grass or a moss-covered fountain, or to listen to a Bach fugue, watch for, wait for, a moment's respite, give up hoping. Then in a blinding flash there is an incredible instant, like the half hour in the Apocalypse when the motionless bird glides in the sky, like that half second that precedes earthquakes—the dogs stop howling, the sea stops rolling in, even the ants stop in their tracks—that unbelievable instant, as brutal as a thunderbolt: the wind falls, all is silent for a second, drops begin to splatter down, messengers of what is to come, and suddenly there is a muffled, uninterrupted hammering, the endless, peaceful stamping of gigantic crowds; the house vibrates gently, a sigh of deliverance mounts from the whole earth, sweetness invades your heart, you want to open yourself wide to the happiness of the earth as it inhales the dampness, to

41

squeeze yourself, hold a hand, meet a friend. In the morning the sea, a dirty red, throws up onto Noria's long beach the carcasses of mules, dead dogs, and uprooted trees, under the forget-me-not fields in the sky.

It was on a morning like that after a night of battle that the second blow came.

Things are opaque and heavy only because of our hardness: they hold themselves in waiting to injure us, to heal us. If we are all tightened up inside, fixated on desires and fears, they're busy only with what they are and preserve their secret. But let consciousness, perhaps inadvertently, relax for a single instant, and open its doors and windows, then liberty floods in like the wind that overturns and uproots, and things, no longer locked within themselves, begin revealing dangerous secrets.

The tall and narrow clock in the vestibule, the only piece of furniture to have survived the shipwreck of the family home, why had it always followed Ramon Rimaz—first to his tiny professor's room at the major seminary, then to his episcopal palace? The clock was waiting for its hour. He had never paid attention to things: he had lived like a poor man, even under the pontifical pomp. The clock had never left him. Had he ever seen it?

After offering mass, he had gone out very early onto the terrace to bathe his face in the cool air, to sniff the bracing odor of the sea, the seaweed, the foam, and the debris that had been washed up. Just as he was penetrating again into the shadow of the vestibule, the motionless pendulum of the tall, narrow clock stopped him short. Doña Paca must have forgotten to wind it. For fun, to use the new forces of the morning, he opened the glass door, slipped his hand behind the blond copper pendulum to reach the key, and was startled to be again making movements he had long forgotten. Then, standing on tiptoe, just as with his raised arm he was inserting the key into the scrollwork clockface, while his left hand gripped the stile of the case, he felt the grain, perhaps perceived a danger, as if, having lived so long among people, the wood had become too attuned to old marks of affection. Before he had given even one turn to the key, the voice of his mother struck him full in the chest.

"Juan, go see what time it is on the church clock."

Whahm, Whahm: the gentle and patient voice of his mother.

Perched on a low chair of woven red straw, her right arm raised, she was supporting herself with her left hand on the stile of the case, her face half turned away. He raced across the tiny square that separated the house from the church; as he came back with the exact time his mother's arm was still raised: *Whahm, Whahm.* Juan Ramon Cardinal Rimaz felt the void that engulfed him, and his arm began to tremble. Leaving the key in the face, he sat down heavily on the chest beside the clock to await the next blow. An intense chill folded him in two, curled him up like a frozen plant. But tiny flashes had begun racing in his limbs, and millions of stars were exploding within him and outside him.

It was perhaps thirty years since she had disappeared: it was only just now that he'd had the revelation of her death. When you lost your mother there was nothing more between death and you, but he had not had the time to realize it. In those days he had been too busy with the rites of death, respecting customs, receiving official condolences, saying the usual words: "No, she hadn't suffered . . . it was better for her . . . in heaven of course," or else, "But yes, that's the way things are, Providence; anyhow, a little sooner or a little later . . ." Entirely concerned with driving a particular evil back into generality so as to render it inoffensive. And this was what was known as faith. He had caught himself calculating the number of years that remained to him should he last as long as his mother. A light wave of optimism stirred within him.

Mama. She had come only once to the archbishop's palace. An unhappy, lost look about her, a sort of terror in her eyes. Countless wrinkles seemed to have independent life on her face, and had dug out shadows around her eyes and temples. Ceremonies and meetings frightened her. She would say, "I'm ashamed." Which meant: I don't know how to sit, what to say. Besides, she was hardly ever willing to leave the family home, except to go on some pilgrimage, to bring back the miraculous water that helps sweeten one's agony. The upholstery, the immense paneled rooms of the episcopal palace, the red hangings, the master canvases, produced endless astonishment in her.

"How can it be? We were . . . and you, because you . . . Is this what the gospel . . . ?"

And he: "To be accepted by the world, the Church has adopted the habits of the world, but there are people like you, mama, and the children, and the saints who are nourished on the . . ."

And she: "You're too smart for me. I'm an ignorant woman."

Nevertheless, it was not his mother's death that had really affected him. Rather, through images of his mother's death, what struck him so powerfully as he stood in front of the clock was the revelation of something indefinable—a void or a fullness, how can one know? So that it seemed to him once again, exactly as when the first blow had struck him at nightfall over the sea, that he could be master of life or death, that all he need do was find the way—but what way?

How I wish I could describe his state of happiness! But did he ever know that he was happy? And I'm condemned to see only from afar, to nourish myself on my own fervor, to demonstrate, to betray with words what was beyond discourse. How can I make you understand that he had gone home, where he found the source from which everything springs? I think of frantic foals, wild sea flowers, wounded evening skies—images with which our feeble hearts play, and that can be found anywhere. But what I want to say is something different. Suppose I were one with the source: the world would spring forth at every second under my gaze and from my hands—how gently and firmly I would advance! But no one is willing to throw me into the pool when the angel is stirring the water. So I go on building houses of words with ancient stones; don't any of you fall asleep in these houses.

But if the lightning hasn't touched you, what can you know, you wise men? Those who have not fallen on the road, under the bullets, those who have not been *lost,* as they say, for days and nights, unable to show a single sign of life, yet retaining a terrible lucidity, hearing everything, interpreting both whispers and silences: "Will you be able to save him, doctor? My God, my God . . ." And the laughter deep down, coming from afar, begins to make something give way. Those who have not suddenly broken free, have never felt torrential life sweep into them with a joy that could burst arteries, or the soul itself, with the dazzling certitude of life; those who have not in a flash been washed clean of the vanities of the world and of its terrors, will understand nothing of what I'm trying to say and will see it only as an idle dream. Let them spare themselves; let them go on eating their bread of dust.

But when he had gotten back to his everyday routine, Juan Ramon was grazed by a furtive regret. All deaths were perhaps blessed. Perhaps the anguish in the eyes of the dying hid a kind of gladness. In emerging from the mother, the baby cries, but does she not at the same instant also feel the excruciating pleasure of living?

Ramon was nevertheless encouraged by the thought that it was presumptuous, perhaps impudent, to cross the passage before his time, since this many-splendored world was offered to him like a promise. It didn't occur to him, he hadn't the effrontery to imagine, that he might take the road reserved for the very greatest, who manage to arrive at unity almost without touching the ground. But how did they avoid egotism? And did they really attain oneness or merely their own ecstatic states? Juan Ramon, still a churchman in his mistrust of exceptional ways, more confident in the way of the humble, in the path of his mother, was thus restrained from indulging in grandiose abstract devotions. Or rather, he imagined nothing, he thought nothing of all that because he had already seen: he saw the sea for the first time, sniffed the perfumes of its wild flowers; the mares, the frantic foals ran by, manes in the wind. All day his mother's voice accompanied him: Juan, *Whahn*. As he emerged into the sunlight of the doorway, the sea was sweeping in, the gulls were calling. A thought came to him: the gulls' wings have aged, airplanes are purer, man improves on nature. He found he was absurd and was pleased. Beneath the sun, already high in the sky, far off beyond the strait, the sea was gray, leaden, and still: he saw it in its truth, an unheard of tumult of light, of innumerable vibrations.

Childhood memories did not submerge him. That is important. He scarcely inhaled the odor of the *albahaca*, sweet basil. The house of his youth was surrounded by *albahaca*. His mother would take several branches in her two hands, then rub them against one another; next she would take her child's face, which she pretended to rumple in her hands like a flower.

> *Green is the albahaca*
> *Green, green, so green*

she would sing.

If the old days had penetrated the open breach with their dreams—like someone who turns around just before leaving and invents a childhood paradise, nourishes himself on blighted illusions after having encouraged himself all his life with stillborn hopes, playing now at being old, humiliating the present so as to veil the fact that the present abolishes him, becoming totally preoccupied with constructing an interior kingdom for the sole purpose of being its absolute monarch—then he too would have indulged in the heart-softening, poetic, and ignoble feeding on oneself that shrivels adults into old men and places old men in their tombs. Nothing would have happened. Juan Ramon would have reassured everybody; he would have been dead, embalmed before being dead. The truth was altogether different: he began to live each day with a child's soul, his former child's soul, which was still intact within an adult's experience. His hope was perhaps reminiscence, but it flew high over the walled gardens of childhood.

Fabulous, the way everything hums, everything teems, everything spills over. Beautiful days in every kind of weather. I thought I was aging, I was asleep, I was talking vapor, dreams, thinking that what was solid had to be external. The mirage has ended, I'm holding onto rock: things vibrate; it's only the gaze that fixes them. I would say, "The sea is blue"—I didn't know what I was saying. I would say, "The gulls"; I thought it was enough to name things. Snatched up, dispossessed of my will and my ideas, I'm pushed around as one is pushed in a crowd, and yet I'm free: movement is born within. I don't walk, I fly. Each moment is bubbling, full, and endless. No more intervals: I exist-with. There is a plenitude, a secret complicity with time that flows, destroys in order to remake; there is an unbelievable joy in being replaced by other living men: a single being, the unhappiness of all is my unhappiness, their happiness is my happiness. Let the child come with the sea. Merché, José-Maria, take each other's hands, you give me the world.

Doña Paca wound the clock. Something had been thrown out of gear—it wouldn't run. The housekeeper said it was the cardinal's fault.

6

⌇⌇

"Will he know how to find his way again?"

"They have their way all prepared in their wings."

"It's like the rockets," the child said.

"Like the rockets," said Ramon.

The child had already disappeared: the red-and-blue spot floated a long time over the sea.

Another day, the child said: "Is it true that the stars in the sky are the eyes of the dead?"

"The poets say things like that, but they are lies. The dead see all things in themselves."

"I know," the child said, "the stars are planets; we'll spend all of death going from one to another of those billions of billions of planets, maybe in rockets."

"Maybe," Ramon said. "Who tells you these things?"

"Minka," the child said, with solemnity and enthusiasm. Then: "They say you're a cardinal."

"Yes," said Ramon.

The child seemed to find that natural.

"My father lives up there," said the child, with a gesture indicating something above the house in the direction of the fort.

But Juan Ramon was not curious.

Toward the end of the morning a woman sometimes emerged out of the boulders in the gully; the child would take her hand. She walked with the long stride of a man, all concentrated within herself, and passed as far from the house as possible on her way back to the Noria road. Had the cardinal recognized the woman who had thrown herself at his feet at the end of the araucaria alleys?

It is only later that their steps will bring them toward each other along the sea, on Noria's long beach.

Merché came with summer. The sailboats of the sea took to dancing. Her face was timid and bold. She was wearing a dress with broad stripes, blue pastel on light gray. The first morning the gulls panicked. But most of the time Merché stayed on the terrace to wait for a letter, a telephone call, to ask herself: Is he sincere? In those days she still ignored the fact that certain questions carry their answer within them: she accorded importance to sincerity, which she confused with truth. Several boys, bored hunters who walked up the gully, came to throw out their chests, leaving their transistors on their shoulders—why go to the trouble when the music and the atmosphere are already there?—before returning to Noria's long beach which swarmed with impatient girls from the big cities. A short time before, Juan Ramon would have grumbled: "*Cretinos, estupidos.*" Now he smiled at life's comings and goings as at the waves and weighed his former virtue. To watch Merché live, that was a big enough happiness. Someone will keep the memory of her long black hair. . . . Souvenirs were given him in advance that he had never had, that did not yet exist in the memory of anyone.

The martin was wasting away. Merché reported that birds' wings had no chance whatever of healing, that a martin should consume every day its own weight in living insects. She was in her first year of medical studies and had just failed some of her examinations, but she knew that much. The child took the martin, climbed all the way up the cliff to give the bird every chance, closed his eyes and turned his face away as he threw it into the wind over the sea. The child had no regrets: he distracted himself by throwing pebbles at green lizards on the other stones, as well as by rescuing birds. Ramon thought everything was fine.

49

Too bad people can't be touched by the child's pity, but it would be more important to have compassion for the child, who soon stopped coming to play in the cove. The police, too, are interested in children. Prudence had required that he be taken back across the border. People didn't know about this till somewhat later.

One day Juan Ramon said: "You are in love."

"Uncle, how did you know?"

She had always taken him for an old fool, a monument, doing what he had to do, saying what people say at that age—in a word, perfectly predictable. He was interesting only because he lived near the sea.

"Uncle, how did you know?"

"The gleam in your eyes. You plant yourself on the ground like a quivering arrow; you hold sweetness in your hands."

Later she was to say that she had seen him then for the first time. His old hands with their long fingers stained with splotches of freckle were closed on the ivory knob. An ironic tenderness rose from the lips to the eyes in that face which was the color of dried figs. He seemed to hide important words behind his lips, as if he had forgotten the useless words that had been employed too often. The link between his thoughts was no longer on the outside but interior, deep inside. You didn't need to understand; you could guess the meaning from the sound of the voice.

"A young girl," he was saying as though talking to himself, "is hard and tender, sparkling, straining toward fulfillment. Brief as dawn. From evasion to weariness. . . . They wait for miracles. I have always distrusted the piety of women. To find God it's better to be happy. . . . The enchantment of love, it seems to me, that must be easy, but full of traps. It is friendship that is difficult."

And she: "Uncle, how did you know?"

All right, she was in love. His name was José-Maria; he didn't like his name. Her family wouldn't hear of it: the boy didn't have the right ideas.

"Good," said the cardinal. José was informed that the way was free. José-Maria had been ruined by Marxist dialectics. He had studied in France, where Parisian bars for refugees had been fatal for him; he had caught the truth, he was contagious. The authorities had withdrawn his passport. He looked at his country from far off.

> *Miña nái miña naicina*
> *eiqui non podo vivir*
> *tanto cura e tanto frade*
> *non teño sitio pramin.*
> *Ay! la la . . .*

sang José-Maria. The country had been handed over to the soldiers, the priests, the leaders of Gloria Dei, to superstition:

> *Curas, militares*
> *Monjas y accionistas,*
> *Y del gloria dei*
> *Y tambien los falangistas*
> *Que turururururururu . . . !!!*

sang José-Maria.

Factories, roads, television sets, a revolution—that's what this country needed. Besides, Russia was becoming bourgeois; Mao's China was the real promised land. As abstract as youth, José arrived with the stubbornness they all have, young bulls full of suspicion, and, if they've been to Catholic schools, with an evasive look for priests. That's because the priests, to speed things up, put the cart before the horse and ruin them for a long time by forcing them to perform acts of piety, inviting them to take part in dull religious ballets before knowing whether faith or love has yet taken root in their hearts. God will recognize His own.

José expected a thousand affectations and was flabbergasted in front of this cardinal, who was usually dressed as a fisherman, talked about neither religion nor morality, and encouraged them to run about in the sierra, to the scandal of Doña Paca.

A starched black wimple banded the housekeeper's long neck up to her ears. The stern face under the white hair was like a flower under a wilted corona. That the niece should live under the same roof as a boy who didn't go to mass, who wasn't even engaged to her, that the cardinal should allow them to go about without any surveillance, all this was beyond understanding. Her eyes scrutinized Juan Ramon's face. She had seen too many of the dying and the dead: perhaps she obscurely wished that her master were a hopeless invalid. The sick can no longer defend themselves against the good you do them. Ramon was not playing according to the rules.

Good Doña Paca, so faithful to the religion she'd been taught. You would say "worker," she heard "Communist," just as she would have thought "Negro—heathen."

"But really, dear Doña, don't you feel that the workers . . . ?"

Her features would become friendly; her eyes would light up with gentleness and comprehension; you were seized by a mad hope.

"But yes," she would say, "of course, only later; the time is not yet ripe"—as she might have said "in a hundred years, in a thousand years."

You no longer have the energy to set her straight. Besides, what good would it do?

For a while it had seemed to Merché that a sort of tenderness was forming in José's soul for her old uncle. One day he had forgotten himself to the point of calling him "uncle." Then he felt guilty: he was forever afraid of being taken in. When the folklore aspects of Christianity are taken away, there are two sorts of people who are especially upset: the good people, whom you deprive of their myths, forcing them to face reality; and the anticlericals, because you take away their target.

José's thrusts at God and religion left the cardinal unmoved. The cardinal refrained from defending that particular god; he was holding God in reserve. Fanaticism lacks humor and looks after itself, thinking it is defending God, who defends himself quite well all alone. Faith flies at a high altitude.

"Uncle," Merché had said, "one thing bothers me about José. He agrees too often—he's always giving in. By loving my dreams he thinks he's loving me, but my dreams are for nobody. He treats me like a little girl; he says he wants to educate me and never stops explaining the world and history to me."

Perhaps Juan Ramon had known that young girls' dreams are nearly as fierce as the ideas of men. That was not a reason to interfere. No one could do anything for anyone. Except be there. That was much more important than people thought.

As evening fell they were alone before the sea. José had spoken again that night with exaltation about China. Merché said she refrained from interfering: it was no longer the words that she heard but her uncle's new tone of friendship. The latter normally avoided all debate and would simply nod his head, saying, "Yes, yes." That night, however, her uncle told the story of the Good Samaritan. José didn't understand it very well. The cardinal, who never gave explanations, made an effort as though he were explaining to himself, hunted for the right words. What Christian societies had been unable to accomplish for the sake of justice and love, or even in enlightened self-interest, why not rejoice when others accomplished it without worrying too much about their reasons, as long as they allowed people to exist humanly? If it's a question of the masses on their knees in the stagnation of destitution or a people standing up erect and in motion, faith sooner or later chose the people on the move. How could Asia, he said, absorbed as she was in her immobile traditions, have any sense of Christianity? Who knows if, by advancing toward her temporal salvation, she might not become more open to the gospel? The Bible was never as strict as those who were well off. In primitive times God hadn't bothered about ethics: the people of the Bible had only discovered the truth little by little through falsehood and violence. The gospel had scarcely begun its journey. Masses of men and women were still at the biblical stage, torn between old false gods and new ones. As for the Church, she no longer had a body: there were only scattered limbs, the remains of a great body formed in other times, wearied by centuries of combat and power in a narrow corner of the universe. Who knows whether another and vaster body wasn't being prepared for her in pain and contradiction, a body that one day she would no longer seek to tame, but to which she would offer her soul intact?

As I listened to Merché's account of events and tried to detect the movements of Juan Ramon's soul, I thought I saw Liang Shang, about whom Martinez Campos had spoken to me, sitting motionless in the great red salon of the episcopal palace.

"So why does Christian civilization claim it's saving itself with the help of atomic bombs?" asked José, who kept up with things by reading the newspapers.

Juan Ramon answered that the good sometimes fought with the arms of evil so as not to see that they sheltered evil in themselves. But attachment was the lot of all, of Christians as well as others. The politicians and the military struggled to maintain provisional equilibrium. This was their work, what they were paid to do; how can we reproach them for that? It was easy to condemn a society in the name of the immaculate ideal that you carried within you. In this way each of us claimed to find in the world outside a truth we hadn't had the courage to experience in ourselves.

Suddenly it was another man who rose up, the cardinal in the pulpit, who spoke solemnly: "My son, the Church sticks close to the ground; she's not made for immaculate consciences that nourish themselves in their purity. For the most part, she prefers what is to a perfection that does not yet exist; she is stubborn in resisting, obstinate, blind perhaps, but like life she leaves the ship only when it sinks. But the time always comes when she goes over to the enemy, to the barbarians, taking her arms and her baggage, because for her there are no enemies, no barbarians; she can believe for a time—moments that can last for centuries—that you spread the faith the way you run a business, setting up foreign branches, calling meetings; she follows behind the armies and the cultural missions, but the hour of truth always strikes when she mounts the cross. Excuse me, I'm beginning to preach—it's the professional hazard. . . . The Church is something else, too: she is humble, I almost forgot that. And furthermore, these words . . . Have you ever heard of Liang Shang?"

It was the last evening. Doña Paca was shaking the dinner bell.

"Start without me," the cardinal said. "I've talked too much; I'm going to walk for a while on the beach."

Because once again Liang Shang was entering the red salon and standing motionless before the cardinal.

They passed Liang Shang back and forth from country to country, from diocese to diocese. A Chinese intellectual who had come from Formosa to Europe on an official mission, he had discovered the gospel and requested baptism: two years later he was a priest. In two years he seemed to have assimilated the scriptural and patristic sources and the whole of theology. From Rome he had been sent to a diocese in south India. With amazement Liang had there discovered a perfectly Westernized Christianity, a caricature. The churches resembled the old basilica in Lourdes; the little girls were even named Lourdes or Fatima; and Indian untouchables were ordained priests, passing without transition from extreme destitution to seminaries where they lived in Western fashion—that is, in luxury—and became lords. Liang had not been able to put up with it.

Once back in Europe, he had led a wandering and impoverished life alone with his faith. A strange thing—is it as strange as all that? Juan Ramon now asks himself—Liang Shang, at first an anti-communist who had thought only in terms of reconquest, after having received the Catholic faith, burned to return to Peking. Perhaps there would be martyrs there—and why not?—but real martyrs, who would be killed for the right reasons.

The little man is now seated in the tall red armchair three steps from the monumental desk, his face closed, ageless, while the cardinal says what it is proper to say: public opinion, prudence, the *gobernador,* the concordat, scandal. The little man stands, takes two steps forward, grows taller, looks the archbishop straight in the eye, and speaks. Not a muscle trembles in his face: "Juan Ramon"—neither Excellency nor Eminence, nothing but the baptismal name; the voice resounds in the immense red salon, hung with the portraits of all those deceased archbishops—"Juan Ramon, are you a successor of the apostles or the director of a corporation?" His eyes fixed on Ramon as if the cardinal were himself the Church, he continued: "You came to preach the cross to us, but you left us to carry it ourselves, and now you curse those who come to our aid without any faith except a human one. I look for apostles, I find diplomats; I thought I would meet servants, I see lords in hieratic poses, Buddhas bent under the weight of their capes, satisfied with their ceremonies."

And Ramon, struck by the authority in this voice, not even thinking of stopping it, saying: "It's what the crowd likes."

"Turn away from the crowd as Christ turned away, not in scorn but in love, so that the crowd can discover in all its truth the mystery behind the spectacles."

The voice is contained, almost friendly. Once again it strikes the cardinal full in the chest; he shivers beside the sea and thinks: it's turning cool—well aware that it's a question of something else. Liang's eyes feared nothing. For eighteen months he had been held in prisons: they had accused him of aiding some revolutionaries. He hadn't wanted a lawyer; his sole defense had been that he asked no one for identity papers and that he had acted in the name of the faith. No one had visited him in prison.

Juan Ramon had stood up, had said wearily: "What should I do?"

Liang Shang had not seemed to understand, even for an instant, that this was a mere formula. He had said:

"Stop believing that public opinion is represented by so-called distinguished people, those privileged by money: in this country the faith could almost get along without God, since it draws its support from the established powers; it is the work, in great part, of flesh and blood. Instead, make sure you see regularly the same number of poor people, workers, and peasants as you do representatives of the middle class; go meet your enemies and listen to them. Speak extemporaneously and stop satisfying yourself by composing abstract and balanced reports after the event that flatten everything out; get away from rhetoric, and pay the price without knowing what it will get you."

What did you do, Ramon? You took his hand in both of yours and led him to the door. He said, "Bless me." You blessed him, satisfied, because he would not make trouble. But the blow had carried. You know well, Ramon, that deep down you have always been on the side of the underdog, but you would say, "What's the use, if I'm alone?" All over the world, everyone was saying: what's the use, if I'm alone? After Liang had gone, you made your way to the oratory. It must have been nine o'clock, the dinner bell echoed in the deserted palace; just like tonight, you said, "Start without me"; you recited a rosary to put your heart to rest. What would it be, to pay the price?

Feeling his way cautiously, Juan Ramon places his foot on the first step of the stone stairs and stands motionless for a moment on the terrace before reentering the house.

Liang Shang must have remained in Ramon's thoughts. How otherwise can one interpret his note to Martinez Campos: "Could you get hold of Liang Shang? Tell him I'd like to pursue a conversation."

That evening was the last of the summer for Merché and José-Maria. It was agreed that they would come back at Easter the following year. The cardinal promised to write and arrange things with Merché's family; he would even make the trip if necessary. But, yes, he would write under the archepiscopal letterhead: he would make use of what authority remained to him. Everything would go well.

7

*B*ecause his sister Concha had loved justice immoderately, the cardinal had to go north earlier than foreseen. This was apparently a piece of luck for Merché and José-Maria.

For the fifteen years since her doctor-husband had died rich, Concha had reigned over the prairies, the vineyards, the scrub, the sheep, and the simple people of her native village. She used to read John of the Cross and Teresa of Avila, and went on building, garnering, sowing, and governing, while looking forward to renunciation. Three times she had attempted to join the Carmelites, three times negotiations had broken down. She would arrive at the monastery making too much of a stir, her head already teeming with reforms. When it came down to it, Concha was posing conditions; in particular, she was refusing to leave her goods to the congregation. Give them up, all right, but not to religion: that would be a bad action for which she would have to account. She had a specific point: it was not only individuals who should take the vow of poverty—that was too easy, since they were already recompensed a hundredfold here below—but also communities. She refused to change her mind. In the meantime, seeing no contradiction whatever between the possession of land and total destitution, she augmented her properties. If someone mentioned to her the incompatibility that seemed to exist between her various enterprises and her Christian sentiments, she replied, "I have no choice; I have to have something to keep me busy."

Her death had been exemplary. For five years Concha had been indulging in legal maneuvers the way someone else might in merrymaking. She needed these squabbles to maintain her health. The mansion she had built above the village was the object of litigation. Concha had brought action against the architect and the builders for faulty construction, abuse of confidence, and embezzlement. The court fees had long since surpassed the cost of the house: she couldn't care less. Furthermore, her claims were well founded, it was said; but in that area, where everybody stuck together, she didn't have a chance. Concha knew it, but her taste for the absolute made her say: "It's not this house I'm worried about—it will hold up longer than I will—but I love justice, I'm setting an example." One night, she went out again to the mansion, this time armed with pick and shovel—an official visit of inspection was to take place the next day, with experts, counterexperts, and judges; she had decided to dig a hole so as to verify for herself the depth of the foundation. In the morning the men of justice found her at the bottom of the hole, dead, her hands clenching the pick handle.

The funeral had been a disappointment. The pastor, at considerable expense, had had a cardinal's canopy moored to the chancel of the church. But the cardinal appeared in black—doubtless the soutane from which Doña Paca had effaced all signs of glory. To the pastor, who was astonished, Juan Ramon gave an answer that allowed for no appeal: he said that sloth alone explained his negligence, that he liked to travel without luggage. So the cardinal sat under the canopy in his surplice. A nameless malaise weighed on the chaplains, the canons, the protonotaries, and unimportant minor prelates; a whole bustling little world adorned in lace, ermine, violet, and amaranth had jumped at the occasion, attracted by the cardinal's presence. A naked man would have shocked them less. Fire from the heavens failed to fall.

The day after the ceremony, Merché had been able to chat with her uncle. Juan Ramon, for the first time, it seemed, had marveled that the funeral ceremony should appear the contrary of what it was supposed to signify. While he had been kneeling on the red velvet cushions, his elbows propped on the comfortable armrests, his head in his hands, strange images had passed through him: he was again vested in his cape, crozier in hand, his miter on his head; he advanced into the nave, raised his right hand toward the choir to stop the Dies Irae, and turned back toward the chancel. "Get rid of these black hangings, the silver tears, the candles with their crepe bows, the crossed tibias, all the bric-a-brac designed to frighten the congregation, take it away. *Fuera.*" The mourners at the wake, between shots of sangria, and later along the route to the church, never stopped moaning: "Such a holy woman, so good; her father was good, her mother was good." He went up to the mourners: "*Fuera!* Get out!" But then, he said, another voice had made itself heard: "It wasn't by changing the decor that you changed the soul. It did no good to shine a light right into people's eyes. A day would come when the gospel would burst its old shell. People would be astonished that so many barbaric customs had grown up out of the depths of fear." For a moment he had again seen the closed face of Liang Shang, and again heard his frightening words:

"Are you aware that millions of men and women, strangers to the faith, move toward death with peace and confidence? You have come bringing us the cross, not the resurrection."

It seemed that Ramon had felt no sadness over Concha's death. Rather, an unfamiliar tenderness, a secret joy at this leave-taking that was so much in keeping with her life—that was, in fact, so logical. She seemed to him to be closer than before. People said that he had a hard heart.

He had accompanied Merché's family on the way back to town. The road went past scenes of his childhood. For a long time, formerly, he had wanted to return to the hedgerows, the poplars, and the fountains of the north. Bulldozers had knocked down so many trees and covered up the old pathways. Tractors went back and forth over the immense expanse of fields. Juan Ramon found this good, felt not a single regret, and was not even aware of it.

It was time to attack, to help the lovers. He had promised. Merché's parents affirmed, like many believers, that faith was a gift, but this declared conviction did not prevent them in any way from relying on something quite different. A bird in the hand is worth two in the bush. A good background, a good education, healthy ideas—that is, theirs—that was all that was needed. At that rate the faith would never have been spread. They were materialists without knowing it. Juan Ramon, who was almost as wary of theology as of dialectics, refrained from theological considerations and suggested to them that it was their daughter, not they, who was getting married; that he, Ramon, would have little esteem for a girl who would let herself be married off by her family; that many marriages blessed by the world had a strange similarity to high-class prostitution; that in addition it sometimes happened that parents helped to manufacture illusory passions which, in an atmosphere of liberty and benevolence, would have disappeared of themselves. These banal words fell from above: they were heeded.

And yet when I returned to Noria almost two years later, the great romance was over and done with. Merché was living alone with Doña Paca in the white villa. A love, enhanced by absence, seemed to have replaced the anxious tenderness to which I had been witness. It was no longer for José that she waited but for the return of the old man, who would perhaps never come back. In any case, I had nothing but Merché's testimony to help me understand not only José's definitive absence but also that of Juan Ramon, who had disappeared a short time after the Altata passion play, while Minka was crossing the border to join the child.

We scarcely ever left the cove. At the hour when the tide entered the gully, we would be walking alone among the gulls, who flew off clumsily at our approach, tracing a circular arc, landing behind us, designing stars in the sand, hopping about, hesitating, and at last taking off halfheartedly, tracing a new arc over the sea. All the while I listened to her voice, by turns timid and imperious, and through the hesitations and silences it seemed to me that I was beginning to understand a little.

Yes, she had thought she'd found an inexhaustible love. The eyes, the voice, the hands of José-Maria made her exist in her own eyes: she had at last thought herself necessary. Fool, she was going to marry to be obliging, out of impatience and boredom. Was it true that many women got married because of cowardice?

José was "Communist" the way her parents had been "devout." Reaction against their little terrors—which they called faith, hope, and love—had led him to rebellion. How difficult it can be to maintain one's intimate truth! People are for or against; they think they are faithful or in opposition, and always courageous. It's a childhood disease that never ends. She had had a favorable prejudice toward everything that was different. An impulse put her on the side of the rebels. She had loved José's insurrection.

No, at no time had she despised him. She wasn't mistaken about others: only about herself. On the contrary, she was very grateful to him. He had taught her how one could fool oneself, mistaking the innocence of pleasure for love, or obstinacy and blindness for courage. Her own sentiments had been reinforced by her family's opposition. Rising up against her family, she had confused self-love with love.

It seemed to have happened this way. Scarcely had he been accepted by the family, thanks to Juan Ramon's intervention—which had ruined what it was intended to secure—than José-Maria began playing the role of conquering organizer. A short time earlier he had wanted to hasten the marriage ceremonies: it was of course necessary to pass through the sacristy, whether one was an atheist or not, since civil marriage did not exist. But once he had entered by the front door into an upper-class family, he insisted on a solemn engagement and a wedding that would break all records. He was prepared for anything: to deny, to promise, to go to confession, to receive communion. Had the Party issued new directives?

At the same time, alone with his fiancée, all at once self-assured and imperious, he believed he had certain rights. His ideal, he naively admitted, had always been to marry a very young girl whom he would form. To his way of thinking this was a sign of strength; he admitted an incurable weakness: he was afraid of a woman who was a complete human being. Suddenly a taste for worldliness, which he pretended to abhor, took hold of him. He wanted to show off his lovely fiancée; he would present her as an object and would rave in public about her clever remarks. Disagreements degenerated into quarrels. To complete the paradox, her family took her fiancé's side: one could no longer call things off, the announcements had already been sent out—what would people think? That had been the end: this love, created by the family's opposition, fell apart with their overhasty agreement. The greatest irony was that José, in a renewal of partisan fervor, had thought he was sacrificing her to the cause. In this way their love, which had begun in one lie, ended in another.

Had she suffered? No. She could have told me the very words that were said, the gestures that accompanied them, the day and the hour when the break had taken place. All this had not been the cause, she said, but the sign. Transparent—he had become transparent for her. For the image of the rebel there had been substituted the reality of the sorry young man in crisis, impatient to succeed. She had gone through this unheard of experience, she said: a being in whose eyes you had drowned yourself became in a flash more foreign than a stranger, while a terrible pity overcame you.

As I listened to her it seemed I recognized a special spirit, a kind of nobility: someone who wanders off, pushes everything out of her way, falls down, but finds her path again. I told her this.

And yet sometimes she would still wonder, as you might puzzle over a distant event that has remained obscure, that never quite made sense. All the efforts that she had thought she had made out of love, sacrifice, and compassion, whether for him or for herself, she said, had produced only brief glimmers of light. You had wanted to give him happy days, give yourselves beautiful memories, you restrained your impatience; yet all of a sudden there is this hideous violence: the words are cruel and open up chasms that you didn't know were there, which perhaps didn't exist before the words created them. How hard it is to live! Should you be silent, or talk things out? You can't give in to your every mood: you hide some things, wipe them away, you think you're being generous, but the violence builds up. How does one know the exact line between telling everything and telling nothing? You didn't want to cause any suffering.

"Most of love's pains are illusory, Merché; they are self-inflicted: moans for what never existed. When love really exists, almost nothing else has any importance, whether it's words or silences. Like faith, it isn't something you lose; you end up realizing that it had been a gift. Certain believers—notice how they worry, how hard they try, and what a good opinion they have of themselves—they say, 'God, God,' because they haven't yet entered into the secret. It's the same way with all those tiresome people who keep bleating about love; they sing of nothing but love in order to console themselves for what they will never know."

"But how do you know if you've found real love, or God, and not just your own inner feelings?"

"Love is its own proof, Merché."

"What do you do in the meantime," she had said, "before the sea comes to take us?"

"Try to be true, without pitying yourself, and refuse all substitutes."

"It's crazy. You're talking like Juan Ramon just before he left," she had said.

"I'm using up all my warmth in words. But you, Merché, you know too much now—so many things to which people attach themselves and which can no longer be of any help to you."

She had raised her gaze above the white villa toward the

lethargic fort: the helmet and the bayonet came and went on the passway between the two towers. She had said:

"Juan Ramon is of great help to me. I too believe that one must go the limit. What is difficult is to keep busy while waiting."

This conversation, which began about love and then switched to God—which perhaps was not really a switch—took place only later, the evening before Merché and Doña Paca had to leave the villa by order of the police. Your most profound thoughts—better to keep them for moments of leave-taking, when you can speak freely, like strangers. Besides, time has nothing to do with this adventure.

8

*M*artinez Campos had not seen Ramon again
since his retirement. He therefore knew nothing
of the cardinal's metamorphosis and learned only by hearsay of
the incredible end of his story. But the fact that such a thing was
possible, and had really happened, threw him into the depths of
reflection.

He had the eyes of a child, the enthusiasm of an adolescent in a
worn-out body: at each visit I had found him stretched out on his
chaise longue. It is twenty years now since Martinez Campos,
secretary-general of the archdiocese, had been condemned to
death by the doctors. Recently he had been forced to give up
accompanying the new archbishop on his travels: a sudden
braking of the car and he would almost collapse; ten minutes on
his feet and his eyes began to spin. An American doctor had
proposed surgery: too much of a luxury. "Besides, on a subject
like this, I'm a probabilist," Campos said; "the success rate is not
yet ten percent; I'm waiting for fifty. By that time I'll be dead, but
it doesn't matter."

His freedom of thought and expression seemed total. Old age
can permit itself anything; the favor that some owed to their age,
he owed to his condition. He could have said or done anything
he pleased—he was going to die tomorrow. But he never did.
"The only one," claimed Padre Albeniz, an old man confined to
the archives, admirably devoid of that universal benevolence that
paralyzes all human relationships, "almost the only one, to my
knowledge, who went to school at the Gregorian, something like

your Saint Cyr, without coming back too serious, businesslike, pontifical, *presumido*—how do you say it in French? He'd seen too much violet, too much red, too many ceremonies. Ambition can go hand in hand with erudition and orthodoxy. The students there were nourished exclusively on theological theses or canon law; their capacity for research into the real, for genuine contact with God and men, was unemployed, and turned into technical and administrative knowledge. They became totally cerebral, while developing a naive desire to exist socially for the greater glory of God. Of course, this is an absolute necessity and, all in all, providential," Padre Albeniz concluded, smiling indulgently. "After all, we have to have leaders. Besides, Saint Paul . . ."

Because he undoubtedly lived by it in depth, Campos didn't always feel the need to speak in the name of truth. This was relaxing. What good was there to keep thinking about the sun? It's enough to know that it lights up people's faces. And similarly, the need to dominate seemed foreign to him. No merit in that: he was a sick man. A robust health, which does not apply itself to the experience of spiritual things, will inevitably drift to more natural and equally necessary realities. Otherwise, who would put up buildings, who would call the meetings, who would bless the sea?

Two office hours from eleven to one, two more in the afternoon from four to six, to add up figures, masses received, masses said, collections received, salaries paid, the balance still due, close all the doors, afix the counterseal of the chancellery on official documents: that made up the greater part of the seques-tered life of Martinez Campos. He spent the rest of his day stretched out on his chaise longue under the immense bay window of his office, surrounded by books from the episcopal palace library; he was the only one to pull any of them out of the dust. Because he had kept himself far from the necessities of action, because he never had to marry his thinking to the real, Martinez's thought had something untamed about it. The eyes flared in his emaciated face while his hands seemed to mold long phrases strewn with parentheses.

Project mobile images on a screen, choose a record almost at random: the spectator will grasp the obvious relationships between the aural and visual images, will find striking counterpoints, whether ironic or dramatic, which he will attribute to skillful calculation. It's the same when we consider a person's entire life, or at least what we can know of it—just as, at the hairpin turns of mountain paths both the valley and the summit gradually grow clearer—in the same way, the continuity and the direction of this life can suddenly appear obvious to us, though all the while we may know perfectly well that it is our consciousness that scents out, chooses, takes hold of one word or one gesture among a thousand others, in order to interpret decisions that may have been due to nothing more than a fleeting mood. This is because we cannot admit that a life has been nothing but a mere succession of impulses, a reflection of circumstances. Our fears and our hopes organize our lives, sometimes in a disabused perspective, dismantling the elementary mechanisms that apparently condition human actions, sometimes imputing them to a providence whose workings we too readily believe we understand. Whether out of indiscreet devotionalism or nihilist reductionism, we fail to grasp the unknown in its unique existence, bound up in inviolable secrecy.

So Martinez Campos, whose evangelical soul was aware both of the mystery of conscience and the ambiguity of human actions, and for whom providence had nothing in common with that deus ex machina that is only another name for hideous fate—Martinez Campos got caught up in the game, sought out, discerned, or gaily invented relationships, heard warnings, and discovered symptoms in the lackluster official life of Juan Ramon Rimaz, archbishop and cardinal. Where everyone else had seen only conformity, routine, and immobility, whether to deplore it, or take satisfaction in it if they identified their master with some potentate of ancient religion, Martinez perceived a warmth beneath the stone mask, a sense of expectation in the immobility, a faith beyond skepticism, and fantasy even in his celebration of church order. To hear Campos talk, had it not been for the humor that gleamed in his eye and said, "Let me do my act," you might have believed that Juan Ramon had passed his life holding back some rebellion, preventing himself from exploding till the day when, having discovered one hardly knows what, a tiny truth of no importance, but which began to grow and finally took over everything, the Grand Inquisitor had at last closed the door.

"But, yes, you know perfectly well," Campos said, "in Dostoevsky, when the prisoner approaches in silence and kisses the inquisitor's bloodless lips, the old man goes to the door, opens it, and says, 'Go away. Don't come back.' Centuries had to pass before he decides to lock himself in."

I can still see Martinez stretched out on his *méridiana*, his head thrown back, his hands nearly translucent in the light of the window (the body is in the shade, the face is in the shade, but the hands above the face are in the light), kneading, sculpting an unknown cardinal, giving him his own thoughts, recovering forgotten images, memories of memories, marveling that he could have been blind for so long, profiting from the occasion that was given him to get away from his books for once, to make, or make over, a living man.

How odd, for example, his first truly personal contact with Ramon. The archbishop had the habit of summoning him over the house phone. The only word that he deigned to pronounce was *subid*, come up. One day Campos had responded drily: "*bueno*." When he had presented himself, the archbishop said, "You are dissatisfied? What are you unhappy about?"

Campos said, "You summon me like a slave. So I answer you accordingly."

Juan Ramon had closed his eyes and remained silent a long time, Campos told me; then he said wearily: "We are accustomed to so much veneration, perhaps servility, that we become hard. It is a pleasure to find someone who resists and doesn't speak from his knees."

70

Afterward they had been almost familiar. In public, however, Ramon had always treated him with a certain offhandedness. He would say: "the artist" or "the philosopher."

In Campos's opinion, Juan Ramon had never lacked humor and had not waited for the last act of his life to prove it. But it was a severely controlled humor that showed itself in a vague gesture, a furtive smile, the flash of a glance. "Like someone," he said, "to whom you posed a question too serious or too personal and who doesn't find the words to respond: the response can be written on his face, overwhelming because unexpressed. Because as soon as you have words at your disposal, conventional and deceitful formulas tend to substitute themselves for the delicacy of an intimate gesture."

And yet cursive phrases had sometimes sprung forth. For instance, in the car that brought them back from that ceremony . . . Oh, yes, it was after the awarding of the Cross of Santiago. Scarcely installed in the back seat of the car, Ramon pointed to the ribbon on his chest, saying: "In my part of the country we sometimes mark trees with a hatchet or a dash of paint—they're the ones to be chopped down, they're already dead."

This car made Campos think of other cars and other ceremonies, as if there had been only one car and one ceremony. . . . And I saw the sumptuous Mercedes glide along next to the steps of the cathedral, and move off as the crowd closed in again: in front, the liveried chauffeur; in back, Campos and the silent Juan Ramon, his face impenetrable, who hadn't unlocked his lips except to say, "Lower the blinds." It was his habit; perhaps he was ashamed to be seen, perhaps he didn't care to see.

It had thus happened that Martinez Campos, either because he had been moved by the eloquence of his superior—but this was unlikely; for Ramon in those days the essential virtue of any speech was its banality: the canon law he had been taught at the seminary hadn't predisposed him to fantasy—or because Martinez wanted to flatter him, although flattery was by no means part of his character; or else because he wanted to sound out the cardinal's resistance, make the pachyderm emerge from his mutism; it had thus happened that Martinez Campos had pronounced several words of admiration: all the while knowing that the archbishop didn't permit one to speak in his presence of anyone's sermons, whether in praise or blame. As if he had already sensed, Campos said, that Christian language was something altogether different from a dissertation, which you could appraise for its coherence, clarity, or lyricism, and that the spoken word could touch only a secret region where it eluded all judgment. Ramon Rimaz had stiffened at first; then an enigmatic smile had lit up his face for an instant, and the phrase had sprung forth, direct, brutal, allowing for no commentary, the tone itself setting the final period:

"Words, words . . . those who speak in pulpits don't know what they are saying. Those who are listening don't listen."

As if he already had some awareness, Martinez continued, that most often everything took place in the world of general ideas, which undoubtedly could help bring people together, whose function was simply to lead them there, but most of them stopped at the formulas so as not to lose their footing. And Martinez Campos suddenly blushed, two red spots marked his cheeks, the diaphanous hands stirred the light, molding interminable phrases, while he gave himself over to his own meditations, which he was at last able to deliver.

Religion, he said, was in the same situation as the general culture in which the world feigned to believe: bookish, mendacious, sterile, something you shoved down the throats of young people either with their consent or by force, as if something that was not verifiable and objective, but intimate and personal, could be the matter of education. There was no doubt whatever that Martinez had been marked by his two years of teaching after leaving the seminary. Real culture, he said, could communicate itself only by existence, one could only live in its presence and be what one was, sensitive to the true and the beautiful, to liberty, so that others might be called upon, from within, to become what they were. Instead, you asked teenagers to compare Tirso de

Molina, Lope de Vega, and Calderón in four pages—or in your country, Corneille and Racine; to write about the passions when they're sixteen years old, or to explain the development of idealism from Plato to Hegel. . . . "They play the game, the little monsters, they're experts at repeating formulas from course manuals, they get used to juggling phrases, masking their ignorance by inventing logical developments."

In this way you taught them to lie in all good faith: it was simply a question of acquiring the technique and realizing that the truth was unimportant; then they were all set for the most brilliant intellectual careers—they knew how to hum the right music. Others would perhaps take away with them a kind of wisdom, which we call humanism, but which can in every way be compared to the wisdom of a concierge; besides, it's pretentious, consisting of a few empty, inoffensive quotations that can be found in every bargain basement, like the rhinestones and cheap jewelry so many women adorn themselves with. It's hardly surprising that more demanding minds trained in scientific method have abandoned this pseudoculture that they mistakenly identify with true humanism. Everything seemed to indicate, he continued with a force that seemed unbelievable in this frail body, that society preferred to neutralize minds, as if it sensed that the truth is dangerous. Someone who has discovered a truth and who, instead of simply playing with it, lets it grow roots, where might he not go? He will become a stranger to his family and his fatherland. Let a man or woman stop manipulating general ideas, let justice scorch them, let the humble truth of human equality germinate in them, then look: they will have become free, a deadly peril.

And it was the same thing when it was a question of Christianity, he said, having only apparently lost the thread of his thought: all too often everything stayed in the world of formulas, of ideas, of sentiments, which in principle should lead to the source, and existed only for that purpose, but which could easily end up taking its place and hiding it. They had trained too many performers, too few seekers. Faith was a presupposition; it proceeded on its own, it didn't cut into our habits like an axe. What is God? What is this, that? Do this, do that, sit down, stand up, all together now. We used to imitate inauthentic feelings, we tried hard, we persuaded ourselves, stopping at the sign without going on to what was signified. We busied outselves in learning and defending certain words; these efforts used up energy that went unused in living.

As if spiritual experience was dangerous, as if this privilege should be left to specialists. And so it sometimes happened that you found the whole show empty; all you could do was blame the world and Satan. As if words, sentiments, or rituals were enough in themselves, comforting us with the satisfaction of having done what had to be done, like someone who scrupulously carries out the various steps of making a fire—arranges the wood, strikes the match, looks in vain for the spark, and then stands up to say, "There's the fire." But what if there is no fire? It's hardly surprising that those trained in experimental methods, pure forms, and direct language turn away when they hear someone say "fire" and see nothing but a heap of wood, hear someone say "spring" and see only the holy water fount, or hear someone say "grace" and see no joy.

Campos's cheeks had become a feverish pink. He drew back his hands, crossed them on his chest, closed his eyes for an instant, and said peacefully: "In my opinion there was no sudden mutation in Juan Ramon. What he became had always lived in him, mixed with I don't know what, with fear, I suppose. Or else he thought he should confine himself to his role, that his hard duty lay there. You see, were he, by some impossibility, to return to work again, he might well conduct himself as he did before. The Church must work out a compromise with . . . let's not go back over all that. You don't expect me to justify the Church: she does that quite well on her own. Wait a minute, something occurs to me—" But it was a huge laugh that shook him until tears came to his eyes. As if he remembered in a flash a whole story of which at first he saw only the burlesque side. And I was seeing Panfilume.

Panfilume was master of ceremonies: Monsignor Ricardo Panfilume, *beneficiato e primo cerimoniere della Basilica Vaticana*. Panfilume had one love: "Pius IX and the Papal Zouaves." That was the title of the lecture with which he had paraded across Europe and the Americas for ten years. He himself joked about it: "There's a clientele for these things, *amigo mio*, retired generals, religious, and seminarians." If you marveled at such perseverance, he would confess: "In Rome I am almost nothing, away from Rome I am important." Impossible to think about Panfilume without thinking immediately of wasps. His obsession was named "wasp." Everything was wasp: hornet, bumble bee, honey bee, even the ordinary fly. At the first buzz, at the first rustle of wings, you had to stop the car, or in a room open the window, and declare open war. Panfilume would cling to your arm: "*una vespa, una vespa . . .*" He didn't even need to see or hear the insect: the mere word *wasp* threw him into a trance.

Jovial, collector of bits of gossip, he would have been the image of happiness if he hadn't from time to time betrayed an incurable melancholy. When you congratulated him on being first master of ceremonies, his horse face fell, his globular eyes stared at the ground, he shrugged his left shoulder, as if to say you didn't understand a thing. He would then raise his right hand to indicate a sense of fate, saying: "I am only number eleven; the ten at Saint John Lateran go ahead of me."

"Patience," you would say, "you will . . ."

"No, no," he would answer, shaking his head, without bitterness, resigned, but with a terrible regret: "The pope's master of ceremonies is always noble; I am not noble."

He was the best of men, Panfilume, nourished in the seraglio, pious and devoted: he piloted Juan Ramon around Rome, he knew the customs, when you should wear the *moirée cappa*, when not, forever correcting a pleat, kissing a ring, lifting a train, or shaking out dust.

And suddenly Martinez Campos, his face grave, after having softened at the recollection of Panfilume, nearly on the verge of forgetting the proof he wished to present, remembered a story:

"Panfilume had just been put in charge of the Hotel X in Pompeii. He had invited us to spend two days there on the occasion of the pilgrimage of the Madonna of the Rosary: he had some minor business to do. What exactly was our prelate's function, what was he doing mixed up in the hotel business? It doesn't matter. Excuse me, it's a silly story, not very good; I'm only telling it to you because . . . Juan Ramon was generous, that's all."

So it seems that the preceding monsignor, director of the hotel, had decided to change the personnel, which was at the time directed by nuns. Several months earlier, in Paris, a contract had been signed with a *maître d'hôtel* of Italian origin, who was himself to hire a cook and several waiters. Panfilume chose to ignore this arrangement and did not consider himself in any way bound by his predecessor's commitment: a courteous man, almost servile with his superiors, he showed himself unyielding with subordinates. On two occasions Martinez and Ramon had been able to see the poor *maître d'hôtel* who, after liquidating his assets, had come with enthusiasm to the Hotel X only to find the door shut in his face; he wasn't even able to find a room or a place where he could leave his baggage. He had been reduced to lying in wait in the street. Panfilume would say: "I don't know you, imposter; *ladro, via, via;* one doesn't approach a cardinal in the street; the police . . ."

And while Martinez Campos related the scene, I was in the immense lobby that morning and could see it all: the glow of the violets and the reds in the flashing of the lights, the shimmering of the fine lace; the bishops, the prelates, and the cardinals as they descended the monumental staircase, still sprightly or already bent over and leaning on young priests, their valets or their secretaries, who were all spruced up and as earnest as airline hostesses—luxury hotels are like theaters; you only need to walk in to feel youself an actor; you throw out your chest, you play the charmer, you are saluted, saluted again, congratulated, blessed, and you end up believing it—discreet smiles of benevolence and authority on their lips; the old ladies scattered about in the lobby under the enormous chandeliers, rising from their easy chairs, moving forward on the thick carpet toward the staircase, all infinitely weary, their faces almost translucent, pained and delighted, a mark of Russian princesses in exile, vacillating silhouettes bending now toward the episcopal ring, the bishop throwing himself slightly backward as if to protest, but yielding his left hand and with the right making a gesture of lifting up again, the Russian princesses stepping back then, collapsing again into their easy chairs.

And Panfilume appearing now on the first landing of the monumental staircase, possessive, fresh, affable, almost hilarious with his Fernandel face, clearly cut out for comic roles; and suddenly his face closing, hardening, the gaze of Martinez Campos following Panfilume's, noticing the man standing against the casing of the revolving door at the entrance, hat in hand. Panfilume advances toward Ramon: "*Scusate, per favore, momentino,*" and he moves off to the revolving door, saying to the man, "*Momentino,*" angling then toward the reception desk, passing through the unsteady Russian princesses like a cyclone, and exactly three minutes later there are two carabinieri, feathers in their hats, and Panfilume is saying: "Expel this man, *out, out* . . ." While Ramon was saying, "What an idiot!" and an instant later, like a moan, "*Dios, dios!*" not even considering the possibility of discussing the business with Panfilume, of convincing him, knowing well from experience that in certain circumstances an insignificant Monsignor could be more powerful than a foreign cardinal, but leaning then toward Martinez and saying, "Fix it up. Borrow fifty thousand lire, go to the police station, give them to the . . . for his trip, his expenses, in compensation for the damages incurred—I'll take care of it."

Martinez then hurrying to the hotel's foreign exchange office, running to the *questura*, and the man pushing away fifty thousand lire, brandishing his contract, shouting that he was going to alert the press, the nuncio, the ambassador, and Martinez saying, "That is your right, but listen to me, the cards are stacked against you, the press, the nuncio, and the ambassador . . . in this country you don't stand a chance," and the man, astonished by this friendly, almost conspiratorial voice, then lowering his head and holding out his hand, while the carabinieri were saying: "*Benissimo, benissimo.*"

But later on, when I'd left Martinez to his repose, his accounts, and his meditations, it was another image of Juan Ramon that accompanied me. Poor Ramon, how many affronts he had had to swallow! Martinez saw him returning much earlier than expected; he was crossing the courtyard of Saint Damazio, a lost look about him, and saying: "A cab, quick; drive, two hours, anywhere." Martinez gave the orders to the cab driver: Piazza Colonna, Via del Tritone, Piazza Barberini, Via Veneto, Villa Borghese, and back by the Piazza del Popolo. I can still see the cardinal motionless in the back of the cab, tears flowing on the face of stone. No one will ever know why. This is a man without a friend. Just as the cab arrives under the pines of the Villa Borghese, right near the *galoppatoio,* I can hear the gentle crunching of the wheels, the horse's almost merry trot, and it is then that Ramon, himself bathed by the freshness of the trees, places his hand on Martinez's arm for a second, saying: "Like a child, he treated me like a child . . ."

What was it all about? Several months earlier there had been a strike, during which the police had charged the demonstrators. Maybe it was about that. There had been a brawl on the square in front of the archbishop's palace. Instinct had won out over prudence: Ramon had gone down. Anyhow, he'd confined himself to asking questions; he had said that violence . . . But the report of a French journalist had been headlines the world over: "CARDINAL HOLDS OFF POLICE AND ARMY."

The *gobernador* had protested. The *presidente* had threatened to cut off certain salaries. . . . Was it about that? Or something else? The *ad limina* visit came at a bad time, that's all.

The two days that followed had been painful. The monsignors had buttoned up. Ramon had passed under icy stares; doors had been closed. Panfilume himself had disappeared. One shortened audience had been enough, a brief flash . . . A single heart, a single soul . . . A foreign cardinal in those days was a mere supernumerary; if he simply tried to take part in the work of the Curia, he promptly discovered that he knew neither the usages nor the tricks: he was a mere provincial at court, an amateur among specialists, a chess player in Moscow. But a cardinal in disgrace was nothing at all.

However, it had been no more than a passing cloud. Time does more than intrigue, and at less expense. The following year, a new pope had received him warmly. It must have been precisely in that year, one happy morning when all business had been completed, that Ramon had stopped short on the piazza to point at Saint Peter's and say: "I had a professor at the Gregorian . . ."

9

~~~~~~

*A*lmost every morning at low tide, after walking past the boulders of the gully, Juan Ramon, in his fisherman's clothes, would walk along the sea on Noria's long, rectilinear beach. A fine day in any weather. What do the hours matter? Bright mornings when the children's cries leap across the sea; honey-thick afternoons when voices fall back to earth and you hear the hum of the silence. Why do you talk about the days getting shorter? Why, when it's still summer, do you think about autumn and winter? Why do you moan that time is passing? Can't you reserve your emotions for more appropriate objects? Ah! if you'd turn them inwards, the world would kneel at your feet.

He went on in this way, his soul unfettered. Each thing continued to give him, in its own time, its simple happiness. How free you are when you no longer see death! At one with everything, the world is no longer outside. How attentive you become: to the movement of your own stride, which sets the earth in motion; to the festoons of foam that the sea arranges on the sand, abandons, takes back, effaces; to the water itself, agitated by innumerable tremblings, in turn exalted, sunken, capricious as smoke, blooming in unbelievable flowers, twisted into spirals, into crooks, raised into tendrils, pacified for an instant at the crossing of the waves that form a tranquil triangle where diamonds drift, its scintillating bubbles like domes, and all this effaced by the next wave, like thoughts that come and go and get nowhere, flame, die out, constantly rise up, only to be vanquished, then resurrected by some force or other; to roots of beach grass scoured clean by the sea, abstract sculptures; to the scattered boulders, fantastic monuments, pure works of the wind, rain, and motion of the sun, as unpredictable as human genius, which keep their meaning to themselves, forever hidden from the mind's curiosity.

People's glances, far from being wounding as they formerly seemed to be, now struck him as friendly. The curve of a shoulder, the form of a face, the grain of a skin, the fullness of the women's breasts, filled him with gladness. He knew that this was not temptation, but a distant tenderness, a sense of friendship with humankind. Temptation had ceased when he had come into power, when his heart had been changed to stone. Petrification— it was the one temptation he hadn't thought of, which no one ever seemed to have thought of. Virtuous, he had thought himself virtuous because he had kept himself far from life. He had put himself into training and had given himself his virtue. Had he detested evil or had he been afraid of hurting himself? When had he cried out for help? To what Zachaeus had he beckoned, when had he eaten with publicans, to what woman, to what prodigal . . . ? To his endless amazement, by discovering the world he entered into the understanding of the gospel.

He had always been surrounded only by men and women who did pious works, who were devoted to the Church—and all too aware of their devotion, serving her but also exploiting her without knowing it: but their little concerns had hidden the world from him. An account book, that was all he had been, he thought, a walking card file, appointing, transferring, standing behind his counter satisfied that he had everything under control, an old horse wearing blinders. He might have died like one of his priests who, it was said, had cried out as he expired: "My records are in order!"

And what was the title of that painting that an overzealous new curate had wanted to stash in the attic? An atheist writer had discovered the canvas by accident in an obscure nook of a church and had written a sarcastic essay about it. You saw a scale: on the right-hand plate, the virtues; on the left, the vices. The needle stood perfectly vertical. High up on the right two owl eyes looked on. At the bottom, this single word: *iqual,* equal. In those days he had seen in this painting only an example of fanciful skepticism, a curiosity, an antique. He had said, "Let's have no trouble with the Fine Arts Commission; it's been there for two centuries, leave it there for a third." And abruptly the revelation was given to him on this beach: he had not understood at all, any more than that mocking writer. The painting was expressing a mystical vision: it could hang in full light in any church. Vices and virtues, it was saying, had almost no importance, except in social terms. A man could just as easily lose himself in his virtues, if he considered himself their proprietor, as a sinner in his vices if he took his pleasure in them. Human virtue, all too human, rendered God useless. He who wounded himself frankly and naively through evil had more occasions to cry out for help. To be healed, you first had to be wounded. That was the drift of Juan Ramon's thoughts, as they formed and faded away with the sea.

At the end of the beach, nine fishermen are hauling in a net. Braced into the cable, their arms are fully extended; the muscles play under the skin, the muscles of the arms, the knotty rolling muscles of the back, and their prominent thigh muscles; the cordage hauled in from the sea makes an ocher heap amid the brown seaweed. When he's reached the end of the line, the last man walks off calmly, his arms hanging loose, seeing nothing; he walks along the column of haulers, advances into the sea, spits into his hands, grips the dripping cable with his left hand: a kick into the sand with his left heel, right hand forward, a kick with the right heel, the muscles of the arms, the thighs, and the back shiver under the oily, almost black skin; old men and young men, pulling together in silence, walk one by one up the column without seeing anything, arched once again. The cardinal—it's as if I could still see him in the memory of another old man. The cardinal looks at his hands. How he would like to move forward, pull, form a single body with their bodies, and get to earn the fish of the sea! He sits down beside an old fisherman on a small boat that had been beached.

"Rain tonight," the man says.

"Yes," says the cardinal. "How do you know?"

"That little chocolate cloud all by itself up there—that's the sign," says the man.

"None too soon," says the cardinal.

"All in all," the man says, "we're in the same boat now. You're retired, they say."

A little later Juan Ramon's throat tightens as he says what he hadn't wanted to say: "Do you believe in . . . ?"

But the man goes on in the same calm voice: "More or less. You never can tell. I go once a month. Keeps my daughter happy."

And warmed up now, speaking as though he were pulling in his words from afar, as if he spoke for everyone, as if he'd been waiting a long time for the chance to speak for them all:

"Priests—can't say we like them any more than we do soldiers or border guards. They all act like they're playing the same role, trying too hard to look like what we're supposed to think they are. It's not their fault, it must be the uniform. Their talk doesn't seem to me meant for us; seems like the women understand, don't know why. Deep down though, they're all right; we like them, along with the blacks, the Chinese, everyone. But it gets you down, it gives you a pain in the stomach, when you think how great it would be if there were fellows who believed in the gospel and all the rest, who wouldn't spend so much time with the big shots, you could meet them easily, to shoot the bull with them, they wouldn't be always asking you, 'Do you go to mass?' 'Don't you go to mass?' or telling you you're good or you're bad, or thinking they're smarter, or I don't know what—yes, it'd be terrific, fellows who aren't always thinking about money or women but seem to be friends with you."

And Juan Ramon, his heart capsized, thunderstruck that

someone is speaking to him man to man, says, "Yes, yes," and tries clumsily to talk about fish, nets, and fishing, before getting up, starting off, beginning the expected blessing, not daring to raise his hand higher, looking for words—friend, brother, son, they all stick to his throat—finally, raising his open hand and saying: "*Salud, hasta mañana.*"

Their paths met along the shore on a day just like that. Perhaps he was first to recognize the woman from the pine grove who had thrown herself at his feet, the one who crossed the cove with long strides, her face closed. In the very same instant he surely saw again the child's face, the black-and-red spot among the boulders. Or else it was Minka who came forward, all fear having left her, as if she had sensed that there was no longer anything but a poor man facing her, who might listen to what she had to say. Minka—I can hear her voice.

"The child has gone back to France."

Her face turns and is raised toward the fortress.

"His father is up there. No, I am not married."

And he, raising his right hand to begin a blessing, smiling as he draws back his hand, as if to say, how does one know what unites a man and a woman in marriage, or outside of marriage, not saying it, but his eyes speak.

It must have been several weeks before the Altata passion play that their paths crossed. It is certain that they were often seen together then, strolling along the beach. I was not at Noria that year. But I can hear her laughter and imagine her leaping into the sea. I see her face as she speaks of her painting. Her voice sounds hoarse, wounded. She says, "A thousand Manolos will not stop me." Her face closes up, and she asks: "Did I have the right to call a halt?" Their strides are coordinated. Was it at that time that he decided to do it? What had he wanted? To save Manolo, thereby going in one swoop infinitely farther than the hopeless request that Minka had made of him, since he knew better than anyone that appeals to the authorities were useless? Or else, having recognized his own joy in Minka's joy . . . Or were José Gonzalez, the visits to the prison, and perhaps the Altata passion play all necessary before he was able to crystallize his decision? These things remain obscure; they will gradually become clearer, to the extent that it is possible to illuminate them without destroying them.

At first Minka seemed to me to be no more than a woman like any other, someone who from time to time emerged from the boulders of the gully, took the child by the hand, and crossed the cove with the long stride of a man in the direction of the Noria road. But I had seen her again for several days on the wide beach. All of my characters will have escaped me—the old man on the second step, Minka, the child—perhaps in order to give me the freedom to dream of them. Could I have known that they would meet? Two years later, when I came back, everything was over.

I owe my meeting with Minka to the Swede. The Swede had fascinated me for several days. His cabin was the one next to Minka's—it was as simple as that. Someone approaches you: it's a smile that comes toward you, or a sadness; you only see afterward the person to whom the smile or the sadness belongs. Adoration precedes her. Like the blind, she was completely concentrated on some secret, or was it that the world hit her with too much force? The next thing you noticed was her superb stride. She was simply made for hiking. She was a Maillol statue—it only occurred to you later to see her as a mortal. She threw herself into the water in a single motion, swam far out, always straight ahead, like someone who is performing an exercise; then, after she came back, having scarcely stretched out on the sand—sleepwalking, you'd have said—she stood up, started walking again, four steps forward, turn, four steps back: she continued the exercise. I knew she was wrestling with something serious. The Swede said: "She makes me dizzy. Must be a schoolteacher, something like that. I hate that kind of woman."

The Swede always talks at the top of his voice; he wants

everyone on the beach to hear him. "I'm speaking to you. . . . Do you know Mexico City? In Mexico City they sell children for almost nothing, you can buy a woman for a few thousand francs. . . ." He was called the King of Noria. Almost an old man, his hair was white at the roots; it was already snowing on the mountain. For the past fifteen years he had spent two months in Noria each year. He had two obsessions: getting a tan and losing weight; and perhaps a third, but he didn't confide in anybody about that. He would flare up, lyrical, fraternal, and cordial, and you would say, "What a character!" A moment later he died down, became skeptical, vain, and all the rest. That's the sort of person the Swede was: an elderly child who talked to conceal a sense of emptiness. When the sun had set, the King of Nordia, with a student cap on his head, would wander through the alleys or climb the narrow streets of the town, usually followed by a pack of children who made fun of him. But the King would turn the mockery to glory; he would enter the shops, throw candy, cigarettes, and even coins into the squealing crowd. Some insinuated that he was deliberately luring them.

One day as the Swede, stretched out on his air mattress, was describing his travels across a picture postcard America, making his way from the Empire State Building to the Chicago stockyards, from the stockyards to Niagara Falls, and was getting ready to cross over into Canada, I left him alone with his lies and said to Minka, "How about taking a walk along the shore? This old fool—I would have thought . . . His stories are terrible."

As we walked toward the sea, she said, "He lacks hypocrisy, that's all it is. He's so poor; don't you see? He's painting his windows.

"His windows on the wall," she said, "like everybody else."

"I don't understand."

"A prisoner in a dungeon, what does he do with his time? He paints. Think of him painting endless doors and windows on his wall. But you can never go through them. Well, we're all busy painting like that. Art itself is less dishonest. Work, technology, progress—create more illusion: you can get rich, travel all over the world, and even get to the planets, but you never pass through the wall. With him, it's America," she said smiling, as if making fun of herself. "As for me, I paint."

"Aren't you the mother of the child?" I asked. "I've seen you in the cove."

"No. He has gone back to France. I'm not married."

"You're running away from something," I said.

"How do you know?"

"You've been with the Carmelites, something like that; or in prison."

She stops, closes her eyes for a moment, then looks at me for the first time. Her eyes are such a bright blue, the cheekbones in her face are so prominent that you want to confess to some sadness you didn't know you had.

"Four steps forward," I said, "turn around, four steps back."

She turns toward the fort: on the passway between the two towers the helmet and the bayonet come and go.

"How easily one gives oneself away! That's what he said to me the first time we met. It was in Toulouse."

Minka was Yugoslavian. I came to know her story little by little as our conversations continued. The war had passed over her, and the peace, which for her had been more war. The Germans had locked her up as a Communist, the Communists as a collaborator. Her father had been shot by the Germans; her mother had been struck down by mistake by the Resistance. In the Ljubljana prison their heads had been shaved, they were undressed, laid out on the cement, whipped, and handed over to the soldiers. At sixteen, when one loved poetry, and had dreams of tenderness . . . They were stamped out, those absurd passions; when she was finally liberated, she had only one thought: flight.

Cross the border in a truck under a pile of crates, hitchhike to Rome, defend herself from charitable drivers, take courses in fine arts, find them insipid, be expelled from Italy, get taken to the

French border, hitchhike to Paris, remain there four days, be escorted back to the Italian border, return again, be taken in charge by the Committee for Aid to Slavic Refugees: that's how the civilized nations have condemned millions of outcasts to destitution or death; many of those who are alive have survived in spite of the law. Finally, obtain a temporary residence permit. keep house for the president of the aid committee, who takes advantage of the situation by not paying her, keep warm at the Museum of Modern Art, be moved by a single desire: to paint. Be unable to buy canvases, brushes, or oils unless she will sell herself for love, but remembers the soldiers at the Ljubljana prison . . . be one day accepted as a model at *La Grande Chaumière* because a girl suddenly fainted, and hold in one's hands a ten-thousand-franc bill.

And then comes a great, naive, crazy idea: I have the right, painting is as necessary to me as bread. Why would she have had any respect for this society that slaughtered men and women, forgot what it had done or allowed to be done, and rushed off again after money? Two furious months: she'd needed two months to assemble in her tiny attic room the five needed plates, the stylets, the inks. This was the idea: make ten-thousand-franc bills just as you'd make woodcuts, but for her, for her alone, and only as many as she'd need in order to eat and to paint. Saint Minka of the easel! She made the rounds of every stationery store in Paris; she knew them all. It was not to be found, the paper used for the bills of the Bank of France, she could testify to that. Finally, she had started. Carve, chisel the five plates, one per color, prepare the papers, ink the plates, find out that the shade isn't right, go off hunting again, try countless mixtures, find the exact color, try the papers, be hungry all the time because she mustn't touch the authentic bill. Succeed at last, at least think so. Eat her fill one night, walk the streets drunk with fatigue, but with a sense of power, when suddenly the unfamiliar fear hits her, knots her throat—not the fear of being caught, which she's used to, but the certainty that she had committed herself to the blind alley of money, that everything she would be able to paint would be only a lie.

Drowned in the market crowds, she had been able to change one of her bills. Alone in the crowd in the middle of rue Lévis, she had known a moment of triumph: she possessed the world. This success had been her ruin, or else had saved her. The mistake had been to present the second bill at the ticket window of a subway station. I can imagine the scene. The Péreire station is deserted. The woman behind the window takes the note, looks severely at Minka, rubs the bill between her right thumb and index finger while with her left hand she turns the pages of a directory, extends her left arm toward the telephone, speaks without taking her eyes off Minka, who stands motionless, fascinated, the idea of running away not even occurring to her, waiting for the two inspectors to arrive, come to the window, take the bill in turn, rub it between thumb and index finger, nod yes, rush at her, box her in. Minka leads them straight to her attic room without even thinking of lying. She says: "Everything's here."

Eighteen months in the Petite Roquette prison. A fall, a winter, the spring, the summer; another fall, a winter, the spring. A courtyard, four trees, women walking in a circle. She had thought she knew and she knew nothing. She had never seen the sunlight. Through the bars of a cell she had seen light for the first time, light, space, the splotches of sunlight rising and falling on tree trunks, painting, caressing, and kindling the leaves, the violet swellings of spring, the gold of fall, the crystalline purity of frosted branches in winter, so many familiar things that she thought she had seen. No one wanted to believe that she had acted alone. She had nothing to say except these few words: "I stole to paint." But finally they became convinced, and with this certitude there grew something like wonder. An expert from the Bank of France had congratulated her on her talent before giving her a lecture. In her last months the director of the prison had let her work in an attic: a woman from some charitable institution had procured for her what she needed.

Previously, she had tried to paint poetically, to prettify everything, as they did at the Academy of Fine Arts. But in that attic something had burst: faces invaded her canvas, masks of lunatics, prisoners, and judges, through the bars among the naked trees. And although to everyone else her works seemed nothing but wounds and cries—for who can understand that happiness is beginning to cry out in the face of the world's misery?—an unbelievable joy starts to live within her. In her first sketches a cross could sometimes be seen in profile through the grill, or springing up from the tortured trees among the masks in delirium: but very quickly she even abandoned the cross, instinctively knowing that she should hide her secret because the wound as well as the joy must be born not out of the representation but of the relationships themselves, out of the painted surface.

In this attic she had known with certainty that she would have neither house nor home. What is the point of having a home if you could be snatched from it? She would bear her country and her law herself. She belonged to the race to come.

The lady from the charitable organization had arranged an exposition for her. Quai aux fleurs. It must have been the wife of a government official, someone like that. Everything had been sold. The city of Paris had acquired a canvas; it must have been a very bad one. The city of Paris buys almost anything.

Her exit from prison had been worthy of Hollywood. Ten steps from the gate a man was waiting for her behind the wheel of a shiny car. He had said: "I've followed your case. Your gimmick is sensational. Work alone—that's the solution. I've got the paper. . . ."

After her visa expired, once again she had to leave Paris, have them forget about her, move south. She found herself in this almost empty bar in Toulouse, which she had entered one evening to wait for a car that was to take her to a deserted village.

There was a huge man leaning on the bar, while the bartender was bending toward him, lowering his voice, saying: "You're crazy to cross with the child." While the child, his face raised, pulled at the man's trousers. After she finished her orangeade, she began to walk back and forth, stopping for a minute to raise the window curtain, starting off again, impatient to arrive in that promised village and begin painting. And he, now holding the child by the hand, the child pulling him toward the door, coming toward her: "You've done time in jail, or what? How long? I recognize them straight off by the way they walk."

They had told each other their stories. His wife had died here in exile. He had said: "I'm going back into the country to help the labor unions—I don't know exactly what's pushing me, desperation or . . ." She had followed him. Was it because of the man, because of the child?

"Did I have the right to make a stop?"

And I imagined this woman, who carried her own law within her, posing the same question to Juan Ramon along the sea: "Did I have the right to make a stop, to bend down for a moment to drink water from the torrent before raising my head again?"

Several days later Manolo Vargas had pronounced words that she now was saying to herself: "You can't give all your attention to being happy." That had touched her more than anything.

"No," he had said, "I have to cross alone. I might be picked up at the border. Do you want to stay with the child?"

Vargas had not been held up at the border, but six months later he had been arrested, locked up, sentenced to twenty years. An impulse had thrown her forward. Once again it had been necessary to whisper with disreputable strangers in order to obtain false papers. It was not a question of rights or of duties. Manolo was in prison. She should be there where he was, with the child, to wait—one didn't know what for.

And she'd been painting ever since. Four hours in the morning, three in the afternoon—a laborer's hours. When fatigue gathered in her legs she knew it was noon; at seven o'clock in the evening the light fell; then she went back through the pines or marched along the shore with her long, manly stride, like someone who is calculating her energy because she knows where she's going.

She painted standing up, in a former stable that the hotel had placed at her disposal, five, seven, ten canvases at once, which made up only a single canvas; you might have said that she painted them on the run, going from one to the other, waiting for the colors to set, lying in wait for the unforeseen accidents of the mixtures or the superimpositions, on the lookout for new relationships, and above all, scraping with her knife, or the wire brush—for example, black colored with Prussian blue and scraped to yield warm gray; like the weather, which corrodes, scours, and reveals; infinitely amazed every time she entered the studio at happy or unhappy developments in the interim. But it sometimes happened that what seemed happy had no future, what seemed unhappy opened a door, as if everything came to be and passed away quite apart from us. It was no longer a question of reproducing nature or of imitating some ideal image of the mind, but rather of cultivating objects as necessary and inexplicable as walls, boulders, or trunks of dead trees that are sculpted by wind, rain, and sea; masks that are scarcely human, just as time engraves faces, forcing them to confess their parentage with stone; strange dwellings in interior spaces, vaulted passageways, narrow streets, patches of darkness, stone coffins for laying out the poor, scaling walls of yellow ocher, burnt sienna, dirty blue, brick ocher, washed brick, dried brick.

She scraped obstinately, leaving the splotches, the scratches, so that her canvases in their final state made you think of ancient frescoes, as if the painter had wanted to renounce beauty, which was too rich and talkative, so as to isolate pure movement; so that from apparently unfinished or defaced objects there would radiate a warmth of forms, a rhythm of joy; you would be unable to say whether it was a birth or a burial, but you wanted to take part. Fascinating, those hieratic masks, whether pained or serene, at the entrance of dwellings, those bent silhouettes amid vast spaces into which you could enter and advance, as in the gigantic canvases of certain masters, that painting of Jean Cousin, for example—*The Marriage of Cana*, which is at the far end of a museum hall, where you like to walk as in a forest on Sunday morning amid the eternity of resurrected forms, this canvas that covers the entire wall by itself, into which you might advance, sit down at the table, or else move past the guests; go lean against the wall at the other end of the room just under the skylight, which itself opens onto a gallery that seems to extend indefinitely, and from there contemplate the table, the faces, the reaching hands, the desert of the museum. As in this canvas of Minka that I'm looking at as I write, sole proof to myself that I haven't dreamed, into which one might advance across the night, wander aimlessly a few steps from the sea: for very high above the walls a tiny white skylight, blue pastel, throws a cry into the dirty ocher, the burnt umber: beyond are the summer, the sea. But no one sees the sea. This faraway, inaccessible flame is Minka, her secret signature on all these canvases over which the businessmen of art will squabble someday, the canvases that she refuses to show, or to sign with her name, that she sells only in order to eat.

"The only glory I really want is that one distant day a few of them will find a place in some museum and someone will label them 'artist unknown.' "

"Well now," I said one day, pointing at the fort, "here you are, attached."

"I have come because he is in prison. A thousand Manolos won't stop me. I must paint in Africa."

But no opportunity ever presented itself. Permission to see the prisoner had been refused her. Only a few notes had been exchanged, thanks to the cupidity of one of the guards. Manolo had ordered that the child be sent back. She believed that even she was in danger. How could she have known that opportunity would advance along the sea?

As every year, the Islands Hotel organized the lecture in its main ballroom. Minka went out of pity. I accompanied her. The lecture was titled "The America from which I Come" and was to be illustrated by Kodachrome slides. The hundred or so vacationers who were in on the secret, not counting the hotel personnel, who turned out in force, gave the Swede a thundering ovation when he mounted the platform, stomach first, his bearing martial and enigmatic, pursing his lips. The shout rang out, "Long live grapefruit!"—because our hero ordered two of them at each meal—but only Arizona grapefruit. The waiters in the restaurant had succeeded in simplifying things by making an ink stamp marked "Arizona." The King of Noria, armed with a long bamboo pole, remained standing for his introduction, after which he sat down behind the projector.

"The voyager who quits the sacred soil of his fatherland for the first time, leaning on the bulwark as he watches the city of his youth fade little by little in the mist, sad at heart, experiences diverse and various emotions . . ."

The applause crackled in a torrent of laughter. At last we were able to continue our route, while "the little waves lovingly licked the steel flanks of the monster," which, an instant later, "were dancing like a nutshell on the untethered billows," and the captain invited "the man who is speaking to you to the table of honor, and placed him on his right. In addition, at each meal we ate lobster and caviar, the champagne kept flowing."

It was fantastic: we laughed till we cried; these absurdities have undoubtedly remained in my memory only because of Minka's laughter, our blended laughter. Once again we were treated to the stockyards, the Empire State Building, the Golden Gate Bridge, the Nevada desert. In the more emotional moments the King stood up in order to give free play to his lyricism.

Remembering a breakdown in the desert, he compared himself "to the poor sailor on the boundless ocean who hangs on to the wreckage with one hand, while with the other he calls out, 'Help, Virgin of Paradise!'" He had seen everything, experienced everything—blacks, Indians, gangsters—had photographed everything; two or three hundred slides had been stolen from him, he suspected the secret police, he had wandered in the savanna, a bison had charged him, he owed his life only to . . .

A slide of the bison was projected, showing his legs in the air—there was delirium. It was set right side up: you could clearly see the bars of a zoo.

We had been able to slip away discreetly, leaving the Swede to his triumphs. We walked on the beach. Minka bent over, took handfuls of diamonds from the sea and let them flow from her hand one by one. I thought it was a kind of coquetry. I spoke to her with the sincere and deceitful sweetness that night encourages: of her marvelous stride, of the adoration that preceded her before her face could even be made out, of the way she had of laughing as she crashed against the waves—her laughter could be heard all the way up the coast to the cape, while the sea foals came up, their manes in the wind, to eat from her hands. A minute later, her face was peaceful again, and her eyes concentrated within. . . . I stopped; there was a second's panic. I thought of the Swede; she must have been listening to me the way she had listened to him.

And she, with her slightly hoarse voice, hesitating as though pursuing some dialogue, instantly effacing—and without even realizing it—all the shoddy poetry of the evening, saying quietly (the way you'd say "It's a pleasant evening" or "The sea is calm") these words, which I am sure I repeat faithfully because they affected me more than I could say:

"Do you know what it's like to be with . . . ?"

"And yet my life . . . ," she continues, speaking to the sea and the night more than to me, "wouldn't it be better to make one's life a work to His glory?

"Juan, is it possible to construct your life's work outside of yourself and keep your own life in His light?"

And I, suddenly capsized, feeling an unfamiliar shiver between my shoulders, made once more a spectator, irremediably outside, began searching for phrases to sum everything up:

"Remember your own words: we paint windows on our walls. These who plunge totally into their soul have nothing more to paint or to write. Perhaps it's better not to fall too fast, but to wait humbly for the angel to point you out with his finger."

"Sometimes," she says, "it seems to me that I am with Him, even in my sins, because I'm waiting for justice."

It was then that I pointed to the fort.

"So here you are, attached," I said: "you love him."

"He is in prison," she said. "Do you know what it's like to be in prison when there's no one waiting for you outside? I'll wait as long as he's in prison. But a thousand Manolos won't stop me." She held out her arm toward the south, over the sea; "I have to paint in Africa."

Saint Minka of the easel! It was then that something clicked in my mind. She was already painting the Africa that she did not yet know. Those masks of lords and poor men, that gnawed, burnt earth—it was the Africa that she had come looking for here, that she carried within her, a world in the process of falling to pieces, of coming to be.

I can now imagine the meetings between Ramon and Minka beside the sea. Perhaps it was some time after he had written, in the notebook that Merché was to find, this phrase, among a dozen others: "To what Zachaeus have I beckoned? to what prodigal . . . ? From what woman have I asked for something to drink?" What is certain is that on several occasions they had been seen together pacing the beach with their long strides. . . .

She pointed to the fort. She said: "No, I am not married." Ramon finally understood what the child had said. Minka spoke of her painting, of Africa. Perhaps Ramon recognized the chant of his own joy.

It is also certain that she had suggested to the cardinal that he solicit the authorities. A letter from Minka had arrived several weeks after her departure. The police had seen it. In it she wrote: "I am safe for the moment. I'm still hoping that your efforts will succeed. I am at a crossroads and I must choose. Why should one love the trees and the color of stones so much, and not the hope of a child? It is harder to make those you love happy than to feel the warmth of great plans. Sometimes I feel the fatigue of being an artist. And still, I'll leave when Manolo returns to the child."

Ramon never received that letter. But he had answered it in advance. The response had infinitely surpassed the request. Had he first tried to get something out of the authorities? When had he made the unbelievable decision? Because it is not enough to want to help. A movement of the soul accomplishes nothing if events don't cooperate with it, like an animal who must get down on his knees for you to mount him.

10

~~~~~~

*W*as Ramon Rimaz suddenly ashamed, one day, of his happiness? Did he want to communicate it? Or was it simply out of weariness that he yielded to the pleading of the local pastor, who had been annoyed for a long time at not being able to show off a cardinal who lived in his parish? Toward the end of the year preceding the climactic event, he was seen in the pulpit of the church at Noria, on the Sundays during Advent. If the cardinal had not returned to active service, he would have lived out his life in peace, and no harm would have come either to Gonzalez or to the director of the prison: it's impossible to do good without hurting someone. On the other hand, Minka and Manolo Vargas would in that case have had nothing to count on except prayer: which is certainly effective, but in a very long-term perspective.

Erect, without making gestures, eyes closed in a mask of stone, speaking to himself, surprising himself with his own thoughts, that's how, after pulling together a few of his old paragraphs from random conferences, I can imagine him in this baroque pulpit over which three chubby pink angels sound the trumpet of judgment. I can also make out the angular face of Juan Gonzalez de la Riva, who sits alone facing the preacher in the raised pew with the red elbow rests, which is reserved for benefactors of the parish. They say one could already feel the hum of silence even before the cardinal had opened his mouth. For it is enough to enter into yourself, at the level where consciences communicate;

everyone feels part of something, even if they don't hear anything. A prince of the church, of course, can say almost anything; the prestige of his robes lends depth to banality. But it couldn't have been that, since Ramon appeared in black and white.

Perhaps he had tried at first to recall some remnants of old sermons that still cluttered his memory: for the words end up assembling themselves on their own; all you need do is call on one for the rest to follow, and you think you're saying something. But by that time mere verbal associations seemed a lie to him; words were at our disposal, but the link between words could only be interior, new each time; truth has to be refired in the depths of a consciousness. Like everyone else, in the old days Juan Ramon would have said: the words don't matter, it's the intention that . . . A smug, pious laziness protected itself in this way, or the "devout" cowardice that repeated, while shuffling the cards, that it was necessary to efface oneself behind the truth—he understood this now as something so obvious it no longer needed reflection, just as he knew instinctively that you could lie while telling the truth, that you always lied when you repeated truth like a lecture, that you had to keep earning it every minute.

He stumbled over the words: long silences punctuated his meditation. But the silence spoke: because you had the sense of a presence, that he was struggling with and against someone. For example, after first speaking of prayer as they usually do—the all-powerful, our nothingness—suddenly stopped by some obstacle, he questioned himself: "Have I the right to pray? For if I pray in a servile way, I am speaking out of another age, I'm transforming God into a potentate, and He will forever be the other. But I am one with Him, neither slave nor servant: His friend." He preached on the absence of God: He left us to our misfortunes; time, sickness, and death were the secret form of His mercy; for in this way we were invited to seek Him in a higher place, beyond our provisional installations; He stopped being a docile marionette at our beck and call.

Defend God? That would be too much presumption. The

Church was not in the business of persuasion. What god were we defending? Besides, for Him, to exist or not to exist was very much the same thing. John of the Cross had said this a long time ago. By denying Him, atheism was still affirming Him, and many believers who shamelessly use Him like a flag deny Him. In some mouths *God*, *faith*, and *grace* could become arrogant words, animated by fear or the taste for power: idols or arms. "One enjoys being a warrior," he said, "counting the victories, the defeats, the wounded and the dead. But the reason we exert ourselves so much against evil is simply to mask it in oursevles. We forget that good is irresistible, that it would be enough to let it germinate, grow within us, take up all the room. . . ."

As far as the Church was concerned, he confessed what he believed: he thought it was enough for her to endure and grow with her word and her sacraments. Yes, nothing was too good for her; she could make a claim on power and prestige: but it was up to the individuals she nourished and educated to exercise the virtues of poverty and humility for themselves. . . . Of course he remained convinced that the Church needed a firm and independent base in order not to dissolve in people's consciousness: there were lots of examples to demonstrate the illusion of those who had wanted to rely solely on their inspiration. But little by little, he said, he had come to think that the social power of the Church could be the cause of its spiritual weakness, just as a mass membership could go hand in hand with profound alienation. The Church itself ought to be poor and humble, without waiting to be crucified. People were able to be poor and humble for themselves, and rich and proud for the Church.

As you can see, the cardinal's homily was not a matter of solemn warnings and abrupt affirmations. His words became as discreet as a feather brushing a windowpane. Then, when Advent was over, he told the pastor that he would no longer mount the pulpit, that he had nothing more to say. Knowledge makes us mute.

The preacher enjoyed a success. Several of the local society women came to congratulate him in the sacristy. They are always the same, all the world over. They understand nothing, but hear the music, find a warmth. It was incurable. Ramon had only scolded them gently. As for the director of the prison, he declared himself enthusiastic. He was a skeptic, on the heavy side, glassy eyed, who spoke with his hand on his heart. He was against capital punishment, against killing people and animals, the subject moved him to tears; he ate meat at every meal. After telling Ramon that he agreed with him on every point, and that he himself might be willing to go even further, he proclaimed that he was a partisan of modern methods of crime prevention. It was generally accepted that prisons inclined people to mysticism; such an opportunity should not be missed. And ultimately this would benefit the common good. He told the cardinal that there was much good to be done, so Juan Ramon went up to the prison.

At the director's invitation and without making any objection, he went there in full dress as an honor to the prisoners. His first words were: we are all sinners. His second: we are all in prison. Some of those who found themselves in this prison might well not have been there; some who were not in prison might well belong there. Had he, Ramon, had the courage to say all that there was to say, he might very well find himself there otherwise than as a visitor. The director's first reaction was to be moved— this was the right approach. But a moment later his amiable skepticism had won out. However, the press had not been there. He said to himself, "What the hell! He's old, like Saint John on Patmos . . . nothing to worry about." This gentle mystic has a sense of humor: the cardinal's contact with the prisoners can only help pacify them in the long run. He insisted, therefore, that on the first Friday of each month the old man come in his cardinal's robes to speak privately with some of his toughest inmates; he issued orders to the effect that the man in red should have every liberty to come and go in the prison as he pleased. This was the mistake of his life. Several months later, toward Pentecost, catastrophe struck. The clever director who wanted to utilize religion to pacify his prisoners was asked to try his methods in a prison of the lowest category.

For his part, Jesu Gonzalez wasn't fooled at all. Of a terrible race: God is their property; like animals of flight, they sense peril faster than the wind itself.

Because his ancestors had made a fortune in Cuba, he lived on eight hundred acres of good land on the other side of Noria among the orange and lemon groves; but in addition he owned three-quarters of the area, not counting the copper mines, in which he employed the poor from the uncultivated lands. At harvest time—a miserable harvest from miserable fields—you could see him stop on the threshing grounds along the roads. He arrived in a Jeep—a young boy, son of the overseer, got out the chair and the *sombrilla;* Gonzalez then sat down, smoked a cigar or sucked on candy while overseeing the mules that turned the mill and the peasants who lifted the straw, sifted, and weighed the grain.

Every Sunday Jesu Gonzalez was present at mass in the raised pew with the red elbow reats across from the pulpit, from where he could oversee both the priest at the altar and the whole congregation. At solemn masses he was incensed: simple mortals must wait till they're in their coffins to receive this honor. Don Jesu Gonzalez sits alone in his pew: his wife died of boredom, his son is an atheist. "He's dead as far as I'm concerned," Gonzalez said. "To be such a devout father, and have an atheist son—what have I done to the good Lord?" Don Jesu was generous, the kind of man of whom it is said: "He is so good; he's a man of such good faith." If you're an atheist, God is not in jeopardy: he retains his chances. If you're a hypocrite, God remains intact, since you're only pretending. But if you're devout, with anguish in your heart at the thought of failing, and you go on accumulating possessions along with your virtues and your merits, so as not to lose everything in the hereafter, then God is abolished. Sons draw their own conclusions. So Jesu Gonzalez found himself in his chateau alone with his worried and feverish faith. It was said that he attended three churches on the first Wednesday in Lent to receive the ashes, and that he received communion several times on Sunday in different churches. To show off, superficial minds concluded; to set a good example, said the others.

Pay a ridiculously low salary to the workers in the mines, call in the police to put down strikes, visit the sick, cover them with kindness, be godfather to the twelfth child of poor families, pay for the seminary studies of sons of his peasants, guarantee a dowry to girls if they entered the convent, pray over the dead—that was Jesu Gonzalez de la Riva, of whom it was whispered that he was one of the pillars of Gloria Dei.

But how can one know who belonged and who didn't? When you said "Gloria Dei," there was always someone to hush you up. Gloria Dei wanted to save Christendom. Its means were simple: piety, virtue, money, power, and military force. The Grand Inquisitor had given himself such an instrument, and his shadow enveloped free men and Christians in a terrible solitude. The movement calls on its members to make retreats, and to practice meditation, chastity, and all the virtues that would make them receptive to the crusade. Because the time for nuances was over: their objectives were to establish an exemplary nation amid the universal disintegration, to influence public opinion, which ought to be simply the expression of divine truths within the collective consciousness, organize, get hold of the levers of power, convert if possible, and reduce whatever can't be absorbed. There could be no coexistence between good and evil: it was the language of the apostles before the crucifixion. Besides, perhaps Gloria Dei was only a myth: that was its strength, like that of the devil. Poor Gonzalez, this was no reason to slash him all over with a knife. But what an idea, to try to play Christ when you own so much property! You can't win on both counts.

It seemed to Jesu Gonzalez, surprised by the new language of the cardinal, panic-stricken in the face of this calm faith, which he did not recognize, and which he sensed could overthrow the foundations of his life, had called in Gloria Dei. Several letters reached the archbishop's palace. Campos has admitted it. He thought that they had had no effect: in high circles they were not at all appreciative, Campos said, of aristocrats who defend the faith along with their lands, or of Gloria Dei which gives lessons to the hierarchy and tries to become its substitute. Nevertheless, it remains possible that Juan Ramon reverted to silence as a result of Gonzalez's maneuvers. But there was worse: a cardinal's sermons were surely not unrelated to the insane idea that pushed Gonzalez to play the crucified Jesus in order once and for all to heal his unhappy conscience, and he played the role so well that it cost him his life. This circumstance itself perhaps contributed to the decision of Juan Ramon, who took another route altogether.

11

Above Altata a winding path mounts to the bald hillock that is called Calvario. Here and there on the threshing grounds, along the path, three cypresses stand rooted, bent by the wind, three women in mourning. These are the stations of the Passion that is reenacted here every Good Friday.

It begins with the trial. The pastor presides in front of the church: he plays Caiphas. The *alcade* plays Pontius Pilate; he is enthroned in front of the Town Hall, belted with a green scarf. Neither the priest nor the mayor wears a mask; their faces are their masks. Neither the police nor the soldiers are hooded: they are in their everyday roles as policemen and soldiers. The false witnesses, the executioners, and the members of the Sanhedrin wear hoods. The condemned man is also hooded: unknown to all, he must remain so. The village priest himself chooses him from among the penitents who come from outside his parish; in penance for their sins, after their Easter confession, they request as a grace the privilege of mounting the cross. Once the man is crucified, he is whisked away into the crowd: the technique has been perfected. The empty cross is not left planted in the ground but is used in making frames, and becomes a door or beam if it doesn't simply feed the fire.

This latter practice was jarring in a country where images of the crucifixion abounded, where crosses were planted in profusion, and where, on religious feast days, monumental statues in wood or plaster representing the scenes of the Passion were drawn through the streets on carts. In this village the characters in the drama were revived each year, made of flesh and blood, both the victim and the executioners, as if to indicate that the Passion did not simply take place in the past.

In the same way, on feast days in some parts of India, after building the statue of their god in clay, after painting it in sumptuous colors, honoring it with flowers and incense, the worshipers throw it into the river, as if the image might veil what it signifies, block the movement of the spirit that it occasions. Perhaps long ago, the religious authorities had wished to spare believers the subtle temptation to use up their emotions by venerating an old story. They reminded them of the fact that everyone was in turn, and perhaps at the same time, Pilate and Caiphas, judge and convict, executioner and victim. The Passion, neither anecdote nor myth, was a mystery that could only be grasped from within, not in the imagination and the welter of feelings, but in the reality of the human condition, fully accepted at each and every second.

As often happens, folklore had just about taken over the proceedings. The Altata Passion was at first sight nothing more than a local festival. Scattered groups sat above the village in the shade of the rocks, drinking, eating, digesting, and sleeping in the pure light facing the sea; grouped around their transistors, they awaited the passage of the procession and the signal for rejoicing. For here, as in other parts of the world to this day, Good Friday inaugurated the joy of Easter. When the condemned man had been hauled up onto the cross, and just as he cried out for the last time, bells rang, fireworks exploded, and the crowds began dancing along the edge of the road, surrendering to all the pleasures of crowds.

The village was deserted: a child cried in the darkness of a house, a chicken began cackling enthusiastically. The whole population was doubtless in the square or dispersed on the heights. The walls of the scabby side streets were pitted and flaked: I thought of Minka's paintings, of the obstinacy with which she scraped, wiped out, muted her colors. An old man with a face of stone, his eyes extinct craters, was sitting in a doorway with his back turned to the street. I asked him the direction: he pointed with his stick. A moment later he turned away and spat violently. When I reached the edge of the square at the highest point of the village, I worked my way through the crowd of simple villagers, miners, gypsies, and tourists in shorts who kept taking pictures.

On the church steps the pastor-Caiphas was enthroned on a purple chair. Disguised by his hood, Jesu Gonzalez, who had fallen at the bottom of the steps was surrounded by soldiers trying to clear a narrow space to isolate the condemned man from the crowd. It was, of course, no longer Gonzalez, and yet as this extraordinary liturgy unfolded it was another Passion that I was following—it was for it that I had come—the Passion of the preceding year, of which Juan Ramon had been a witness and Jesu Gonzalez the real victim. A witness stepped out from the group of hooded men, mounted several steps, and shouted: "He has said that he would destroy the temple and build it up again."

"What have you to say?" said the priest, who was wearing his true face. He was bending over his papers: you saw no more than his shiny skull; he was reciting his lesson—he would never cast off his role.

And it was as though I could still see him—because in my innocence, some time earlier, I had believed he could help me understand Juan Ramon's adventure—in that room that was so abandoned and funereal that you were afraid a wisp of wind would be enough to cause everything to crumble into powder: the dirty statuettes, the discolored artificial flowers, the dusty books, and all the baroque furniture. It reminded me of those funeral chambers, which are sometimes entire palaces, that have been brought to light by excavation; they say that a single opening, a mere breath, can turn them to dust—the horseman, the horse, the chariot, the king, the queen, and all their suite. In the same way, I saw him moored to his desk, bending over it, his face in the yellowed papers; his waxed skull, rubbed, glittering, appeared in full light. He finally finished rummaging in the old papers and stood up brandishing a newspaper clipping. His voice reached me from far off.

I watched him, this faithful and devoted priest, fade back into the throng of apologists of what is, of the knights of a common sense that has already petrified into sterile virtue. Woe to the one who wakes up, steps out of his definition; may he be shut up in an asylum, may he be crucified, may he be shot at with words and even bullets—and let's keep it to ourselves. His voice reached me from far off: "We, that is to say, the authorities, in full agreement . . . smother the affair, higher interest." Juan Ramon had wished to retire to a monastery to prepare himself for . . . "That's all." The priest stood up suddenly, inflamed by the anger that a lie unleashes in you when you get tangled up in it; he said: "My friend, leave Ramon and Gonzalez in peace, I have informed the authorities. I must warn you, in your own interest, you ought to . . ."

The man was silent.
"Tell us if you are the Christ," Caiphas was saying.
"You have said it," replied the man.
"He has blasphemed!" shouted the priest as he stood up inflamed by anger, while he pretended to tear his surplice.
Shouts arose from the crowd: "To death, to death! *A la horca!*" You couldn't be sure whether the shouts were intended for Caiphas or the defendant. A line of hoods encircled the condemned man, hands slapped him, as the voice of the priest was drowned in the tumult:
"It is in your interest that one man should die for the whole people."
The crowd boiled in a blaze of color and movement. A man raised his leather gourd, threw back his head, ecstatic, and the red

jet of the sangria streamed into his throat. Soldiers pushed into the crowd, which fell back. The condemned man crossed the square to the podium on which the *alcade* stood waiting, belted in green, wearing his own face; he shouted:

"What shall I do with your Jesus?"

The crowd roared: "To death—*a la horca!*"

Pilate washed his hands. I heard: "*Sucio,*" that is, pig. Without being able to tell whether the cry was intended for Pilate or for the condemned man. The crowd rustled with the movement of multicolored fans, like a tidal wave of drifting faces. Their glances weary, their eyes disappointed or curious—the faces of children sucking candy, of tourists adjusting their cameras, of villagers drinking wine. While cries of hate rose with such violence, or of derisive laughter so abrasive that you could hardly think of them as simply part of a role—rather, it seemed they were expressing a real hatred, a true mockery, although it was impossible to tell who or what was their object, the condemned man or the judges, the role or those who played it, the staging or the reality that it signified—I also saw faces in prayer that had a kinship to death and in themselves justified the whole masquerade. There was one especially, a motionless young soldier, his eyes closed, who let himself be carried along by the movement: holding his rosary in his two hands, his fingers still, he was illuminated by the sweetness and majesty of death; I would have liked to shake him by the shoulder and say to him: "What are you able to see in this?"

But another face was already appearing beyond the crowd, a face of stone with closed eyes. It was Juan Ramon Rimaz in his fisherman's clothes, walking among the poor who had seen all this, and heard the shouts, a year earlier. And I could imagine him wounded by this shameless fair that transformed a secret into a spectacle—unless, as a stranger to all this, the idea was continuing to grow within him while, already powerless to put himself on the right side, to wallow in sentiment, he heard himself pronouncing outside of time the words of Pilate as he washed his hands. . . . Why had he, Ramon, every time the *presidente* or the *gobernador* approved and applauded, declaring that one should judge people simply in terms of the higher interests of the nation, why had he not risen up? Why had he always yielded, for laudable motives, to the *raison d'état*?

They had dressed him up in the red cloak and crowned him with reeds over the hood. Two men began to drive in the crown; the man collapsed. A soldier advanced toward the executioners and gestured: no, no. They stood the condemned man on his feet, put a long bamboo pole in his left hand. The hooded men then bowed down to him, holding their coats to their chests with their left hands, while with the right they made a ceremonious gesture. Next they began to spit in his face, real spittle, frothy, that dripped down along the hood.

The truth was in the game. All those who bowed down too low before the great of this world were preparing the violence of the slaves: violence for violence, an infernal circle. Power and all the prestige that accompanied it—Jesus had crucified them. How could those who had governed in his name have been able to act like princes, to cover themselves with all those emblems of glory that had been flouted once and for all, that had become the privilege of the world? Or should one expect to see the outrage renewed in each generation so that the truth of things will remain perceptible? The truth is in the game, Ramon thought as the square emptied, as the crowd went off to position itself along the way, as the procession—the victim who dragged his cross, the hooded ones, Pilate and Caiphas, who had become spectators, and the soldiers who formed the escort—started to climb the winding path to the calvary. It would advance from station to station, halting for a moment on each threshing ground near the three cypresses, while at the same time clusters of tourists would leave the shade of the rocks to gather along the path, and would follow the crowd across the stones and the cactus, so that three movements would be forming simultaneously: the crucified and his cortege, surrounded by the soldiers in the dust of the path, and on each side the two frayed columns of spectators.

110

The soldiers who escorted the victim had considerable difficulty in isolating him from the crowd. Some men would push through the guard, hold up the cross for an instant to relieve the convict; in contrast, others would shove him; pious women would rush forward to kiss the wood. The soldiers would push them all off: contrary to tradition, it was said.

But these furtive women who brushed the sacred wood with their lips forced me to recall another spectacle, the Good Friday way of the cross in Jerusalem. I had followed it myself and so could visualize what Martinez Campos had described to me of the pilgrimage to the Holy Land he had made with his master years earlier. The cortège moved along in the narrow streets that mount to Golgotha: twenty or thirty men (there were too many of them, they got in one another's way)—white, black, Franciscans, two cabinet ministers (it was whispered in wonder), and several bishops—carried on their shoulders a long black cross. The crowd was packed along the route; everyone wanted to touch the cross, to kiss it. Campos admitted that he had been deeply moved and had had great difficulty in holding back his tears. He had turned to Ramon with a gesture toward the procession. He had said: "Shouldn't we, too?"

Juan Ramon's gaze had become icy. He hadn't relaxed for a second during the ceremony. He had answered: "No." Campos had been shocked, but now he said: "I was a child, I was indulging in cheap emotions, believing they rendered glory to God; it's a pleasure like any other. I am certain now that Ramon was lost in meditation, that he was following another passion. He was amazed there were so many people who dared to carry the cross in symbol and ceremony, whereas during those days in Jerusalem almost everyone fled, and in the everyday reality of things, almost everyone was still fleeing and no longer even realized it."

But here the condemned man, though protected by the soldiers, was enduring real suffering. Did Juan Ramon have some inkling of the perfect crime that was being carried out before thousands of eyes? The rumor circulated to the effect that Jesu Gonzalez had been covered with countless wounds, sharp and deep. According to Merché, who reported the whispered talk, it might have happened this way: someone had guessed that Gonzalez de la Riva would play Christ, someone who had been able to follow him, spy on him when he had gone one night to open his sick soul to the priest, perhaps to negotiate the privilege of carrying the cross, in order to liquidate, once and for all, the anxiety he felt about his salvation, all the while continuing to live as lord and master. The weapon could have been a stiletto, a knife cleverly disguised in a fist. Was it one man who had inflicted the wounds or had there been several? It might have been a worker who had been fired from the mines, a union official who had been imprisoned, anybody. No one would ever know, since the order had been given to hush up the affair. But the fact that a year later a line of soldiers was there to protect the condemned man could be taken as an indication of proof.

The man who was to be crucified this year was bearing up well: they were now laying him on the wood, they were about to tie his hands and his feet: afterward they would haul him up. He would then cry out: that would be the signal. What did this fake victim matter—he would have his dinner tonight and sleep in his own bed! Nevertheless, he'd shown pluck, this year's Christ, to dare to be Gonzalez's successor. For a moment it occurred to me that a policeman might have been wearing a hood as a disguise in order to unmask the assassin. Sure, that's it!

Poor Gonzalez! Last year's convict moaned and fell in a heap. Maybe they thought that he was laying it on, overplaying his role. The last stations had been skipped. The hooded man had taken up the cross, had carried the man who was to be crucified up to the place of execution. They had doubtless come to realize that something was wrong. This wasn't on the program, but the show had to go on.

I imagined Juan Gonzalez de la Riva under his hood losing his blood, hate in his heart perhaps for the one or several whom he might have suspected or could even name. He is tempted to drop that cross right there, tear off his hood, and point a finger at a face: assassin! Or perhaps, refusing to flinch, driven by shame to heroism, he is wholly taken up with suppressing his moans. Or perhaps, acquiring all at once a superhuman grandeur, passing over from play and complacency to reality, forgetting his divided soul that had been totally engaged in fighting fixed battles so as to hide the deception from himself, he becomes, by grace, humble and poor, one with Him under this cross. Unless, deprived of all will, consciousness having by now abandoned him, he is already in the peace of God, who welcomes all those who struggle.

I was moved by an absurd tenderness for Jesu Gonzalez, who suddenly appeared to me as an adventurer of the soul. What a fine impression we give, we who are so pure and truth loving, when we shrug our shoulders at these sad friends of God! Seeing in us and outside of us nothing but mediocrity and lukewarmness, we are mere spectators, sitting in the referee's chair in order to count the punches. Our wisdom and purity are more sterile than their lies or their errors.

They finally raised the cross. "Come down and we'll believe in you," the hooded men shouted, who were now hurrying everything. It was then that the crucified man collapsed completely: his feet slipped on their support, one of his hands came out of the cords, the body swung to one side and floated grotesquely, held by a single arm: and as he fell loose, his hood, caught on a snag of wood, had been torn: for a moment the face of Jesu Gonzalez appeared in full view, but so soiled and deformed that those who recognized it doubted their eyes. But there was no question of spoiling the party. The pastor had shouted the cry that the crucified man had been unable to give. A flag was brandished as for the start of a race: firecrackers exploded, the village bells rose in tumult, effigies of the *alcade* and the pastor soared above the crowd, monstrous dolls that exploded in the midst of laughter and applause. The crowd began singing the Alleluia, dancing had already started on the threshing grounds along the path. Death was absorbed by life as Jesu Gonzalez de la Riva was whisked away.

That Juan Ramon himself had noticed anything was, in the final analysis, highly unlikely; he was doubtless alerted only by the rumors.

Merché and José-Maria, coming down from the sierra, had taken the detour via Altata. "The *corrida* is coming to an end," José had said.

And she: "Don't laugh, your laugh grates, try to understand. Wait—look!" Just as the firecrackers and the effigies were exploding, as the bells rang from the roofs of the village, as the dead, enveloped in white shrouds, sprang forth from among the boulders to the delight of the crowd, they had been able, for an instant, to catch sight of Ramon's face above the mob. He was like a blind man, Merché said, letting himself be pushed along in the crowd. It was then that a red flag had been raised, and they heard the first notes of the "*Internationale*." But the *Riego* hymn had been the stronger. Before the soldiers charged, they had been able to make out the first stanza:

> *Si los curas y las monjas supieran,*
> *La paliza les iban a dar*
> *Subirian al coro cantando*
> *Libertad! Libertad! Libertad!*

Perhaps on that day too, under an almost pink sky, the martins were turning in the evening, shrieking and slicing the air's softness with their hard wings. They must have been martins in transit, migrating south. Far out on the sea a single white sail spun around.

Merché and José-Maria had seen the cardinal again. They had lingered a while in the crowd. José despised dancing, he saw alienation everywhere; so they contented themselves with watching the dancers on the threshing grounds. They came back down

114

to the cove in silence. The night had gone to sleep on the sea. They were not holding hands: all day long quarrels had alternated with tender sentiments. Nothing to worry about: as you already know, their quarrels have been settled now for a long time—time carries away disputes along with our hours of happiness.

"Don't you see the lie?" José said. "They're amusing themselves with religion. They're expecting from God what they should demand of their own courage."

"That's not the point," Merché said. "Courage can change the world, but who will change the hearts of people?"

"Change the world and you change people," said José.

"You make people simply a product of things. Your men who change the world, you imagine them to be pure, disinterested, almost saints. Besides, I can't stand perfect students; can't you be simple, and just love what exists?"

The argument ends as usual: "Bourgeoise, you little bourgeoise."

Juan Ramon's tall silhouette stood out before them. Ten steps forward, he stopped short, facing the sea; ten steps farther, he stopped again. Merché had known that Ramon shouldn't be disturbed: she had wanted to make a detour. José had laughed in a certain way. Later, when the cardinal had made his strange decision, she often heard that laugh: and at the same time she saw again the tall, motionless silhouette. It was perhaps this laugh that had helped to detach her.

While I myself was coming back down along the sea, evening was polishing the stones. "This has happened for some reason," I said to myself. The sea breathed gently. From time to time a high wave would charge, lifted up by some unknown nightmare; a peaceful splashing would then set in again. This had happened for some reason.

Perhaps it was that very night, a night like this one, on this same path, that Juan Ramon Rimaz had known what he would do.

12

*A*t the sound of the car, Doña Paca once again lifted the curtain. First, she saw a foot, which was emerging from the ancient automobile. . . . The old prison chauffeur had been refusing to leave the wheel for some time now—they were all lazy good-for-nothings . . . then, the red soutane, which protruded from under the black *cappa,* and then as the cardinal stood up, the hat with the gold tassels. What an idea, to put himself out for those thieves, workers, and Communists in the prison! The right flap of the *cappa* was thrown over his left shoulder and hid the lower part of his face. Juan Ramon advanced with too lively a step. The old woman knew then in a flash. Terror knotted her throat. The shocking steps advanced into the vestibule, mounted the stairs, and headed for the room without hesitation, as if they had always known it. The steps now came and went on the mosaic, from the wardrobe to the bed, from the bed to the wardrobe; they were descending the stairs—heaven's angels protect us!—and suddenly the man was there, in the cardinal's fishing clothes. A young face, friendly, slightly ironic, Manolo Vargas, while Doña Paca, fascinated, saw only one thing: the pastoral ring that the man was still wearing on his finger. She was about to cry out. Manolo said: "Shut up, grandma." He made the same gesture that Ramon had made the first time he'd gone out without his hat, when she had called to him. "You haven't seen anything. Everything went fine, the guards got down on one knee, the chauffeur was snoozing, no rear view in the jalopy—that was luck. You haven't seen a thing, grandma; your boss's orders, don't try to understand. I wanted to knock him out, that would have got him off, but he said no, and told me to keep the ring. Got his whole life to think about it. Anyway, I'm taking off, I've got my passage. *Salud.*"

What have they done with Juan Ramon? The official version was that the cardinal had retired to a monastery to devote himself to meditation, prepare for death, and receive the care that his advanced age required. This was the version that the local pastor had communicated to me. But Ramon had never been in better health and had no need of a monastery in order to meditate. Should one believe the rumor? The governor was supposed to have said: "He is in prison: let him stay there. Let him be forgotten. Let him say his prayers."

The police have given the order to close the house. Doubtless because of the flowers. Doña Paca and Merché are getting ready to leave. Once a week a hand lays three purple roses on the threshold of the white villa, on the side facing the sea. There is someone here whom no one knows. The police have come, secretly, to interrogate. Paca claims there are men lying in watch at dawn among the boulders.

Seven o'clock in the evening, once again. This is the terrible hour here. After traversing the gully, the sea covers the cove, comes to lick the first of the stone stairs. The sun falls behind the islands; one would say it has gone to have a drink. The gulls have gone away, the voices are dying down; the men and women who come and go on the Altata path are no more than shadows, the dead who are passing. As the sun sinks, a splotch of light dances and mounts the mast of a ship above the boulders of the gully.

"In your opinion, Merché, why did he do it?"

"I believe—for no reason. He was beyond all explanations. Someone needed him. He went there naively. Or else, maybe your friend Martinez was right: Juan Ramon never did lack a sense of humor. Unless . . ."

How quietly the light mounts the ship's mast! You would like to pray for the light to stop. But you shouldn't. Dawn is breaking on other shores.